I0545067

Claiming Abby

Club Isola 3

Avery Gale

CLAIMING ABBY
Copyright © 2013 by Avery Gale
ISBN: 978-1-944472-71-9
Print Edition
First Publication: October 2013

ALL RIGHTS RESERVED: This literary work may not be reproduced or transmitted in any form or by any means, including electronic or photographic reproduction, in whole or in part, without express written permission.

All characters and events in this book are fictitious. Any resemblance to actual persons living or dead is strictly coincidental.

Chapter 1

ABBY GARRETT STRUGGLED to consciousness even though a very large part of her mind wanted nothing more than to float back into the dark, empty escape of sleep, but there was something pulling her up through the sludge into awareness and beckoning her to think clearly. She knew her mind wasn't working as it should. She was struggling to form coherent thoughts, but for some reason, she knew she couldn't afford the luxury of sliding back into blissful slumber. Sleep was dangerous, but she didn't know why.

Once she finally managed to open her eyes, she was surrounded by the strangest darkness she'd ever experienced. There were two small circles of red light glowing in front of her, and when she started reaching around her, she quickly discovered she was in some sort of box. When she had been about eight years old, she'd watched a movie about a young girl who had been buried alive by kidnappers. Ever since that night, she'd been absolutely terrified of the idea of being shut inside anything remotely enclosed and dark.

Trying desperately to tamp down her rising panic, Abby instinctively reached for the panic alarm on the bracelet her brother and his techno-brilliant, billionaire boss had given her for security reasons. When she realized the bracelet was gone, she felt herself sliding even deeper into fear. Forcing herself to take several deep breaths, she was able to bring her focus back enough to realize she was in the trunk of a car, and what had been a fairly smooth ride suddenly become much bumpier. The change probably meant they'd left a main road and were now moving over rough terrain. Abby reached for her earrings, knowing they held a secondary alarm system she'd sworn to Jace was totally over the top and unnecessary. Her brother had been a Navy SEAL, and to say that he and his teammates were a bit over-protective of her was an understatement of Biblical proportions. When she realized her earrings were missing as well, she had to stifle her terrified scream.

Abby immediately started working her fingers over the inside of the trunk's top, searching for the latch. She knew most cars had an interior release, and as long as she hadn't been locked away by some low-rent asshats driving a beater, she had a good chance of being able to open the trunk from the inside. She had to fight her rising panic and the urge to try to remember exactly how she'd come to be in this mess because she couldn't afford the distraction.

Her best chance of surviving was to focus her energy on getting safely out the trunk before the driver reached his or her destination. She'd have plenty of time later for a stroll down memory lane to figure out exactly how this had come to be... right now, getting the trunk lid open, then getting out without getting run over by another car or seen by her captors was going to require all her focus.

Releasing the latch turned out to be fairly simple, but holding on to the trunk lid after she'd unlatched it turned out to be a much bigger challenge. Abby was tiny by anyone's standards, hell she was barely five feet tall and rarely weighed over ninety-five pounds. She had spent years taking self-defense classes, but it didn't seem to matter how quick she was or how precisely she could place a well-timed kick to the groin. The simple fact was the lid was bouncing as the car made its way over the rocky and uneven terrain, and each bounce was pulling her further into the air.

Abby quickly ran her free hand over her clothing and was relieved to find she was wearing warm-ups and a hoodie, and she still had on her running shoes. When she felt the car begin to slow down and saw the turn signal begin to flash, she knew this was probably her best shot. Raising the lid just enough to slip out, she rolled out and hit the ground with a thud before sprinting into the dense trees lining the dirt road. It was dusk, and the trees cast a deep enough shadow, she hoped the driver wouldn't immediately notice his trunk lid was now bouncing freely in the air. The rapidly encroaching darkness had its disadvantages as well. Within minutes, she could barely see her hand in front of her face, and since she didn't have any idea where she was, she knew better than to just take off running. *Hell, who knows what kind of holes, ditches, or canyons might lie in these trees.*

She had only recently gotten the all clear to start running again following the surgery she had almost a year earlier. When she'd been hurt skiing in Colorado, Jace and Ian had insisted she be flown to New York, so a Club Isola member—who also happened to be one of the country's best orthopedic surgeons—could perform the delicate piecing together of the jigsaw puzzle pieces of her broken leg and mangled knee. Their actions had seemed *over the top*, even for them, but when it came to Abby, her older brother had always been her knight in shining armor.

Jace had saved her life when they'd both been much

younger. She'd been inadvertently exposed to penicillin while helping her dads work calves one spring and collapsed in the yard, suffering from anaphylactic shock as she'd tried to return to the house. Had Jace not seen her fall, they'd have never gotten her to the hospital in time.

Abby had been enjoying her last afternoon of skiing in Aspen when she'd been bulldozed down the mountain by a beginning snowboarder who had fallen further up the mountain and rolled into her. The man had been twice Abby's size, so when he'd become a human snowball tumbling down the slope, he'd managed to send his board careening into Abby's left leg. She still had nightmares about the sound of her femur being shattered and the blinding pain of her knee disintegrating. Unfortunately, a rapidly approaching storm had meant the only way off the mountain was in the back of a snow-cat. The ride was so rough, the pain had finally overwhelmed her, and she'd simply passed out.

She'd spent almost ten months dividing her time between her work for Garrett Oil and a rehabilitation unit where she endured torture sessions at the hands of a sadist disguised as a physical therapist. Even though she'd never admit it, right now, she was awfully grateful her therapist had been such a jerk because, despite the odd warming sensation she was beginning to feel in her leg, she was still running without much effort and certainly without the pain she would have felt had she not worked with Teryn the Torturer.

Returning her thoughts and focus to maneuvering over the rugged ground, Abby tried to stay as parallel to the roadway as possible. She might be a Mensa member, but she had to have one of the worst senses of directions of any human on the planet, so following the road was the only way she knew she wasn't just traveling in a circle.

Her parents loved to tell the story about the time she'd gotten lost in her own backyard after dark. They'd teased her unmercifully about it, but they'd also installed a system of accent lighting that could be "adjusted" to the point she'd wondered if pilots ever mistook the paths in their yard for a runway.

Cursing herself for the flash of fear that kept skimming just below the surface, Abby made a conscious effort to once again bring her thoughts back to the here and now. She'd spent many nights sitting around the fire pit in her parents' backyard, listening to Jace and his team members talk about their various missions. The one thing she'd heard them say time and again when they'd been mourning the loss of a friend or teammate was getting caught up in fear or letting themselves become distracted was usually what had made the difference between life and death.

Abby knew concentrating on her escape was the best way for her to stay focused on the task at hand, and right now, her escape depended on her ability to put as much distance as possible between her and whoever had been driving that car.

Face it, Abby, if their intentions had been honorable, they wouldn't have locked you in the fucking trunk.

KALEN BLACK HAD just started his shift working in the security control center on the small island owned by billionaire Ian McGregor. Kalen had joined the McGregor Holdings security team after retiring from the SEALs. He and his best friend Logan Douglas had both been recruited by their former team leader, Jace Garrett.

It hadn't been a difficult decision for him because he'd been both physically and emotionally drained after years of seeing only the worst of humanity. Kalen had spent years studying the writings of the religious leaders and mystics, and the longer he worked for Uncle Sam, the more difficult it had become for him to see where the gun in his hand was any different from the one clasped just as tightly in his opponent's grasp.

Kalen had just pressed the remote, opening the door for his best friend and former teammate, Logan "Boomer" Douglas when an alarm sounded, alerting them Jace's younger sister Abby's primary security system had just gone off-line. Kalen and Logan had only recently made their interest in their friend's younger sister known. They'd fought their attraction to her for years because of her age, but each time they visited the Garretts' Texas ranch, their desire to claim the little tigress had grown until there just hadn't been any way to hide it any longer. Logan's voice sounded from the chair next to him.

"That's Abby's primary alarm, right? Anybody remind her about changing the batteries recently?"

"Yes it is, and I don't know. I'd intended to mention it to her when we saw her a couple of weeks ago, but after the clusterfuck with Holly, I didn't get a chance to even say goodbye, let alone ask about batteries." Both he and Logan had been disappointed they hadn't gotten to spend a few extra days with Abby at the ranch, but Jace and Gage had needed their help protecting their new wife, so they'd flown back to New York the morning after their friends' wedding and commitment ceremony. "I just got the go-ahead from Jace via text message to activate her secondary locator."

Typing the commands quickly into one of the computers in front of him, Kalen frowned at the screen when he got an error message similar to the one he'd gotten when Abby's bracelet had stopped pinging on their screen. Every member of their security team, all of Ian's personal administrative staff, and his new wife, Callie had jewelry that continually broadcast their current location to the staff in the security control room. After Callie had been attacked, Ian had gone all out to design and manufacture devices easily mistaken for high-end pieces of jewelry and expensive watches rather than high tech audio and GPS transmission devices. Kalen figured the patents alone were probably making Ian and his co-creators several million dollars a year.

"Send another message to Jace, we've got a problem. I hacked Abby's cell phone carrier, and I can't get a ping from her phone either. I want to activate the chip, but per protocol, we need his or Ian's go-ahead." Kalen saw Logan's fingers flying over the keyboard in a blur. *Damn, he can even type faster than Grayson.*

Mitch Grayson was one of their counterparts at The ShadowDance Club in Colorado and was a computer geek of the first order. They'd all been in the Special Forces and had known each other for several years, so they enjoyed the way their paths often crossed since Ian McGregor and the owners of The ShadowDance Club, Alex and Zach Lamont were long-time friends.

Kalen had already set everything up so all he had to do was push a single key to activate the small chip Abby's surgeon had slipped in among the myriad of hardware they'd put in her leg last year. Christ, just thinking about the injury she'd sustained made Kalen's stomach flip over. When Abby had been hurt, he and Logan had been halfway around the world, helping the ShadowDance team bring home a couple of kids who'd been kidnapped by their nanny and her money hungry boyfriend. By the time they'd been wheels down on U.S. soil, she'd already been moved to a rehabilitation center in Texas.

Any thoughts of Abby being in danger sent cold chills racing up Kalen's spine. She was without question the most beautiful woman he'd ever known. She'd inherited her mother's Native American grace and beauty, but she'd gotten her brilliance and affinity for the energy industry from her fathers. It was a commonly known *secret* Jace and Abby's parents were involved in a polyamorous relationship.

The damned seconds seemed to drag as they waited for the go-ahead from her older brother. Something deep in his gut was shouting at Kalen that Abby was in trouble, and in another minute, he was going to proceed without her brother's word. Kalen's fingers had already been moving to press the button when he heard Logan's phone beep, and his friend simply say, "Go."

Chapter 2

ABBY COULD FEEL the branches of the trees tearing at the skin on her face and arms. For some reason, the darkness surrounding her seemed to amplify everything, or perhaps her mind was using that to ground itself against the tidal wave of terror she was fighting now that the adrenaline that fueled her escape was starting to ebb slowly away.

She kept thinking about Kalen Black and Logan Douglas, remembering their afternoon at the pool behind her parents' home. She'd known her brother and Gage let them spirit her away so they could spend time with Holly, but there had been a lot more to that afternoon than simply distracting her. For some reason, Abby knew most of what had happened had been about testing the waters and finding out how she would react to their obvious interest in her than it had been about her brother's privacy.

An almost hysterical laugh threatened to escape her lips before she managed to pull it back. Just the idea of those two Doms *wondering* anything was absurd. Kalen and Logan were among the most balanced and self-assured men she'd ever met. As for wondering about her reaction to their interest... well, that was just plain dim-witted on their part. If they didn't know by now that she had been insanely attracted to them since she was barely a teenager... they just plain hadn't been paying attention.

Abby had been academically advanced for her age, finishing her first Ph.D. when she was eighteen, then completed the second one a year later. But being smart sure didn't mean she'd been emotionally mature. As a matter of fact, the opposite was probably more accurate. She'd been immersed so completely in the sheltered world of academia, she'd rarely dated or even spent much time with the opposite sex, aside from her conversations with her brother's friends.

Abby suddenly realized her mind was wandering again, so she shook her head as if that physical action alone could clear the cloudiness that kept creeping into her head. Why was she feeling so muddled? It was only then the bone-deep cold she'd previously managed to ignore crashed through her, threatening to drop her in her tracks.

Stopping to catch her breath and get her bearings, Abby listened and was relieved when she didn't hear anyone chasing her. She squinted into the darkness, trying to make out any identifying landmark that might give her some clue where she was. The last thing she remembered was leaving the gym near the hotel where she'd been staying in Washington D.C. and feeling like she'd been stung by a bee.

Knowing she must have been drugged scared the hell out of Abby. She quickly ran her hands over her body, making sure all of her clothing was where it was supposed to be. Knowing someone had had their hands on her while she hadn't been conscious turned her stomach, and for a few seconds, she was afraid she was going to throw up.

Since she had only flown into town this afternoon, she wondered how they'd found her so quickly. Hell, she hadn't even taken time to unpack her bag before heading to the gym. She was supposed to meet with members of the Senate Energy Committee tomorrow morning, so obviously, someone didn't want her to share her recent breakthroughs in the areas of biofuels and renewable energy sources. Abby hadn't intended to tell them everything she'd found—not just yet, anyway—she hadn't worked out all the kinks. But she certainly had enough to share—just her preliminary notes had set off alarms with members of the Middle Eastern Energy Consortium.

She had planned to call her brother, telling him she was "in the neighborhood" after her meeting tomorrow. She knew she was being a coward by waiting, but she'd also been convinced Jace would alert Kalen and Logan... so she'd stalled. She hadn't been sure she was ready for all that meeting with them would entail, so waiting had seemed like a good plan at the time. *Not so bright, Abby. Maybe if you had done the right thing, you wouldn't be in this damned mess.*

It hadn't taken her eyes long to adjust to the darkness, but she was still grateful the full moon could be used to her advantage. Taking stock of her surroundings, Abby was relieved to see that it didn't appear they'd taken her far. Judging by the trees and rocks she was seeing, she didn't think she'd even been taken out of the state which meant she was probably in the mountains of western Virginia. Just knowing it wouldn't take her brother long to get to her if she could find someone willing to help her contact him was comforting... knowing he would almost certainly bring Kalen and Logan along... not so much.

KALEN HAD ABBY'S chip activated and was mapping it

before Jace even made it to the control center. "Talk to me." The worry in his voice was evident, but Kalen was impressed that his friend seemed to be making a huge effort to stay in professional mode.

"I've got her on the map, and I'm overlaying the latest satellite images now. She had been moving at a steady speed in a northwesterly direction—approximately forty miles per hour, but that abruptly changed a few minutes ago. She reversed directions and is probably averaging two to three miles per hour over mountainous terrain, so I doubt she is out there training on purpose." Kalen wanted Jace's opinion, so he waited until his friend and boss could process the information. Kalen was sure Jace would draw the same conclusion he and Logan had, and he didn't have to wait long.

"She's gotten away from whoever had her, but I doubt she was prepared for the weather up there, and that cold front we were watching has already hit that area."

Kalen wasn't surprised Jace knew the security team had been closely monitoring the incoming storm. Nobody wanted Club Isola members getting stranded on the small island and being forced to call their coworkers to explain why they wouldn't be able to make it into their offices Monday morning.

"Fuck, we need to get to her before they find her again or she..." Kalen knew exactly what his friend hadn't been able to finish saying. Unless Abby was dressed in some seriously warm weather gear, she was probably already feeling the effects of hypothermia.

Logan was already on the phone, and from his end of the conversation, it was obvious he was talking to someone at the airport. Jace was speaking with Gage, giving him a quick update and letting him and Holly know he wouldn't be returning to their small apartment inside the club anytime soon. While both of his friends were busy making phone calls, Kalen couldn't take his eyes off the small flashing dot on his screen—as if keeping his eyes on the cursor indicating Abby's position would keep her from slipping away from them.

It couldn't happen again. They just couldn't lose another woman in their care. Their last mission as SEALS had been to rescue a young woman who had been kidnapped by rebels, hoping to extort money from her wealthy Saudi cousins. Her family hadn't wanted to pay the ransom, and by the time Kalen and Logan's team found her, she'd been raped and beaten to death.

The thought of losing the one woman he and Logan had longed to make their own was almost enough to scramble the last of his control. It was Logan's voice that brought him back from the edge he'd been so close to going over.

"We have ten minutes to gear up and meet at the chopper. Tony will be here in thirty seconds to relieve us." Kalen grabbed three handheld GPS trackers, quickly powered them up, and synched them to Abby's tracking chip. They'd already donned an impressive amount of gear and were seated in Ian's helicopter as it lifted off in under seven minutes.

Under different circumstances, Kalen would have been damned impressed with what all they'd done in a few short minutes, but with Abby's life hanging in the balance, it felt like they'd spent too much time grabbing medical supplies he hoped like hell they weren't going to need.

Andrews had been the closest military base with a helicopter capable of maneuvering in the mountains in the rapidly deteriorating conditions, and it had only taken one call from Ian to ensure their transport had been set up and ready to fly by the time they set down. They quickly transferred their equipment into the larger helicopter and were off the ground in less than five minutes. Their time in the air was used to set up their gear so they could fast rope down as close to Abby's current location as possible. When the door on the side of the chopper slid open, the frigid wind nearly took Kalen's breath away, and his fear for Abby shot straight off the chart.

Chapter 3

I T WAS PAINFULLY obvious the weather was deteriorating rapidly, and Abby knew her only hope for surviving was to figure out some way to make sure she was sheltered from the moisture that was starting to fall. The temperatures had dropped significantly since she'd started running back down the mountain, and that meant the light misting rain that had started falling a few minutes earlier was going to turn to sleet in short order. Just when she was about to give up and crawl under one of the larger pine trees lining the road, Abby spotted the burned remains of a small building. There wasn't anything left of the small structure, but there was an open-front, low-ceilinged wooden shed that looked like it might at one time been used to keep wood dry for use in the tiny cabin.

Shaking out a musty-smelling canvas tarp laying inside, Abby tried to erase her footprints with a branch she managed to tear loose from a tree several yards beyond her hiding spot. She threw the small branch aside and backed into the small shelter and pulled the awful smelling cover over her head and tried not to identify the odors emanating from the offending piece of fabric she hoped would keep her out of the sight of anyone tracking her. Abby knew she'd have a better chance of her body heating the smaller space.

Keeping her mind busy was going to be a struggle because Abby had already been exhausted from traveling and the grueling workout she'd just completed before she'd woken up in the trunk of a damned car. Add to that running through the trees over uneven terrain, and then looking for this small hidey-hole had claimed the last of her energy.

Trying to sort through what her kidnappers might have had planned for her was important because it might give her some idea of who she was hiding from. She knew the Consortium wanted her bio-energy project results because they would have a hard time refuting or duplicating information they didn't have time to study. She'd bet they had already raided her hotel suite and taken her laptop. She smiled to herself, thinking how surprised they'd be it didn't even have a password. There wasn't any need for any security to protect the small computer she used for keeping up with her friends from college and exchanging pictures. The most interesting thing on the small unit was the videos she'd been studying from various do-it-yourself home improvement shows. Abby had never been the least bit interested in cooking, but she loved remodeling and woodworking.

She hadn't kept anything work-related on her personal computer for several years. Her PowerPoint presentation for tomorrow's meeting and all her research was saved in her personal folder on Garrett Oil's secure server. She was suddenly very grateful her fathers had listened to their long-time friend and colleague, Daniel Lamont when he'd suggested they work with Colt Matthews and Mitch Grayson to set up a system Mitch had told them was more secure than the Pentagon's.

Abby knew that she had to fight back the exhaustion

and sleep tempting her with its siren call of a blissful escape from her current predicament. Instead of being lulled by the taunting of her rapidly stiffening muscles, she worked to stay focused, using her memories of that warm afternoon by the pool with Kalen and Logan as a blessed distraction. If she really let herself sink into it, she could almost feel the sunshine caressing her bare skin as she basked in the warmth it had provided. After she dived in the pool, she'd felt the water surge around her as both men closed ranks quickly. She'd known there wasn't any way for her to outswim a couple of former SEALs, but with her head start, she'd gotten almost to the other end before they caught up with her.

They'd led her quickly up the steps in the shallow end and into one of the more private areas surrounding the open area of the pool itself. They'd made short work of her skimpy bikini, and their dual looks of appreciation after they'd stripped her had been a huge boost for her ego. The bright sun had been pleasantly warm, and Abby had been grateful for the plush towel Kalen draped over the large rock they'd laid her on. Kalen had lowered his lips to hers in a kiss that went from sweet to conquering in under five seconds.

Abby had been so lost in Kalen's smoldering kiss, she hadn't noticed when Logan spread her legs wide until his mouth sealed itself over her waxed pussy. She'd screamed into Kalen's mouth and felt Logan's chuckle against the ultra-sensitive lips of her labia. Abby had never been completely waxed before and had been astonished at how much more sensitive she was to their touch. Between them, they had sent her over the edge, making her come three times before they'd wrapped her up in the towel, then led her up the outside stairs to the small deck running the width of her bedroom. They'd both kissed her sweetly and promised better things were to come once Jace, Gage, and Holly left the next day.

Knowing they had planned to spend a few days with her had been the only thing that had kept her from sobbing like a child denied a treat when Jace told her the next morning he was pulling them in as backup because they'd gotten information that her new sister-in-law was in danger. Proof once again, fame was a double-edged sword. The morning sun had barely started peaking above the horizon when Jace had found her sitting by the pool. When he'd begun their conversation with an apology, she'd barely fought off her tears.

Suddenly, Abby heard a soft snap that sounded like a wet twig breaking under a footstep. She held her breath for so long, she was starting to feel faint when she heard the scuff of a boot and knew whoever it was, they were standing just outside the small shelter she was hiding in. Just as panic started to overtake her, she heard a familiar voice call her name, and the relief that washed through her was so overwhelming, it felt like it had taken her muscles hours rather than seconds to respond. Throwing the foul-smelling tarp aside, Abby launched herself into the waiting arms of Kalen Black.

She heard him grunt out a breath as she hit his chest, and when she wrapped her legs around his waist and locked her arms around his neck, she felt his arms tighten around her as he pressed his face against the side of her neck. His whispered, "Thank God" was the only thing she heard before she let the tears flow freely down her frozen cheeks.

THEY'D FAST-ROPED DOWN into a small clearing about a quarter mile from the last signal they'd gotten from Abby's chip. With the possibility of a short signal delay, they knew they couldn't pinpoint her exact location if she started moving again, but just before they'd reached the mountain, the cursor had seemed to stall out in one location. Kalen had sent up a silent prayer that she had found shelter rather than been injured or worse. He'd taken the most treacherous path because if she'd already died from exposure, neither he nor Logan had wanted her brother to be the one to find her.

When he'd seen the low-roofed woodshed, he'd tried to approach it as quietly as possible since they didn't have any way to know who else might be tracking her out here in the freezing ass rain. The bottom line was she might be here because she wanted to be. All of their assumptions about an abduction had been exactly that—assumptions. Until they knew for sure who or what they were dealing with, they had to assume the worst-case scenario. As he'd been making his way to the small shelter, he'd noticed a tarp in the corner. He knew he could move with complete stealth if he needed to, but he'd grabbed a small twig with one hand and snapped it while keeping his weapon clasped tightly in his other hand, holding it alongside his leg.

At the muffled snap of the damp twig, Kalen heard a small gasp from under the tarp, and his knees had nearly buckled in relief. When he'd softly called her name, there had been a couple of seconds' delay before she had thrown off the tarp and sprung into his arms. She hit him directly in his chest with her small body, and he'd nearly fallen over backward at the force. Later... much, much later... he might see some humor in that fact, but right now, all he could think of was how grateful he was to have her in his arms.

Securing his weapon, he tapped his communication device and let Jace and Logan know his location, and that he'd found her. He hadn't even tried to get a blanket over her because he simply didn't want to let go of her long enough to dig it out of his pack. He could hear Logan running toward them and knew Jace couldn't be far behind.

As he held her tight against his chest, he felt the moment she let go, and her gut-wrenching sobs tore at his heart. He'd rescued a lot of victims and knew they often held it together until they felt safe enough to let go, and it was only then the tidal wave of emotion came crashing out. Kalen had always been amazed at the strength of the people he'd rescued. He'd seen them hang on for days as their rescue team led them out of jungles or over miles of barren sand dunes without shedding a tear until they were safe in the arms of someone they loved and trusted.

Knowing Abby had let go the minute he'd wrapped his arms around her filled Kalen with hope that her heart already trusted him even though he knew the real battle was going to be with that brilliant mind of hers.

Chapter 4

L OGAN HAD ONLY been a few yards from Kalen when he'd heard him say he had found Abby, but honest to God, it had taken him a full five seconds to overcome his heart-stopping relief and get the muscles in his legs to respond. When he'd run up to them and seen Abby wrapped tightly around Kalen, he knew his friend wasn't even going to try to set her down to wrap her in the heat-insulating gear they'd packed. Instead, Logan stepped up behind her, pressing his body against hers while he shook out a thermal blanket that looked more like a giant piece of aluminum foil than a blanket, then carefully stepped back so he could wrap it around her.

When Logan started tucking the blanket in around her, she turned her tear-stained face to look at him, and his heart missed several beats. Even with her eyes red from crying and mud and blood smears over the scratches on her face, she was still breathtakingly beautiful. When she leaned into him, Logan dropped everything he had in his hands and held his jacket open. He almost growled in satisfaction when she hadn't hesitated to scramble inside his coat and wrap her tiny self around him as tight as the bark on a tree. He enclosed her in the jacket and was happy to have Kalen's help zipping her securely inside.

For several seconds, Logan just stood still and held her

tightly against his chest. Being able to feel her heart beating against his own—knowing they'd found her alive and well—was staggering. Logan felt his heart swell as it was filled with a soul-deep sense of gratitude for every single person who had worked to make sure they'd made it to her in time.

If he was honest with himself, he would admit holding her was more for his own comfort than for hers, but he didn't care. It hadn't taken her but a few seconds to wiggle herself into position and settle against him. Christ, she was nearly frozen. If they'd been forced to wait out the storm, the outcome would likely have been much different.

Logan had known she was operating on pure instinct, her body was seeking warmth. When he'd leaned close to her ear and whispered, "Take off your shirt and bra, baby," she had moved quickly to comply. Thank God she was petite and agile enough, she didn't have any trouble shedding her wet clothing. After she'd stuffed the wet clothing in one of the pockets lining the inside of his jacket, he'd directed her to pull his shirts up, so they'd be skin to skin.

Kalen had shaken his head and chuckled when it became obvious she wasn't coming back out of the warmth she'd found inside his coat. Logan watched as Kalen rolled the blanket back up and picked up both packs. They started quickly making their way back the way they'd come.

Logan had been happy to feel Abby's bare breasts press against his naked chest. Her nipples were like sharp icicles—hell, they felt like they could almost pierce his skin. The first press of her frigid skin against his own had almost stolen his breath, but he'd somehow managed to hold back the flinch and shiver that had almost been reflex. He'd been convinced she would have pulled away if she'd thought she was causing him any discomfort, and Logan knew Abby was right where she needed to be—for both their sakes.

"Baby, we're going to meet up with your brother in about ten seconds. If you don't want him to see you naked from the waist up, I suggest you stay right where you are." Logan would have sworn it wouldn't have been possible for Abby to get any closer to him without having his cock buried deep inside her rapidly rewarming body, but he would have been wrong. At his words, she wiggled closer, then sighed softly when she found a position that seemed to suit her.

Logan had barely finished talking when Jace ran around the corner, his eyes going wide as he quickly took in this situation. Her brother stroked the back of her head several times in a move that was obviously familiar to Abby because she hummed against him. When Logan looked up at Jace, the man's deep love for his younger sister was clearly reflected in his eyes, but there was something else there as well. It was as if Jace had silently passed the torch to his two friends. Jace hadn't made any move to take her from Logan, he'd only asked if she was injured, then quickly pulled out his phone and begun making calls.

They'd directed Tony Dent to have the local authorities on standby, and Logan knew EMS was probably already on the road waiting for them. Logan hoped like hell there would be enough transportation available all three of them would be able to accompany Abby to the local hospital for evaluation. Logan was determined he and Kalen would accompany her even if it meant kicking out one of the paramedics. He knew it was important Abby rely on them equally, and that meant both of them sticking close to her. Everything he'd ever learned about D/s relationships preached beginning as you intended to go, so Logan felt strongly they needed to both be equally involved in her care.

Logan looked over and saw his friend shaking his head and smiling. Jace was still talking on his phone, so Kalen had leaned close and said, "I'm fairly certain you'll be riding in the ambulance whether the paramedics like the idea or not. I'm sure as hell not going to help them peel her off you, and I doubt Jace will be foolish enough to try it either. Christ, only someone who hasn't ever seen our little Native American Tinkerbell in warrior-mode would be willing to take that risk." Logan agreed, and he appreciated Kalen's attempt to lighten the mood a bit.

Any doubts Logan had held about transportation had been quickly extinguished when they'd rounded the last corner and entered the small clearing that had been designated as their rendezvous location. They'd been blinded by a seizure-inducing sea of flashing lights. Raising his hand to shield his eyes, he glanced at Jace and smiled. "Ian?"

"You have to ask? Who else do you know that could pull this together in under two hours? Hell, you know it takes big money and highly placed connections to get a response like this on such short notice, let alone in this weather."

Logan was relieved to see Jace finally looking like he was actually breathing again, and Logan knew it had to be killing him to stand by and watch as Logan kept Abby tucked securely inside his coat. But Jace had regularly touched her cheeks and brushed her sodden hair out of her eyes. It was obvious that his friend continually needed to reassure himself that his little sister was indeed safe.

THE FLOOD OF relief Jace felt when he heard Kalen say he'd found Abby had caused his knees to buckle, and he'd found himself leaning against a tree to keep from folding face first onto the sodden ground. He'd waited until he'd seen her for himself before he'd called his parents to let them know they had found her, and she would be fine. He'd called Holly and Gage next. Holly's elation was like a warm hug to his soul.

"Are you alright, husband mine?" Her sweet inquiry had felt like a band tightening around his chest. She'd been thrilled they'd found Abby in time, but somehow, she had known the price he'd paid—how personally responsible he'd felt when he found out Abby had gone off-grid.

He couldn't help but wonder if this would never have happened if he had left Kalen and Logan in Texas with Abby after the wedding. Perhaps they could have gotten her to open up to them about the trouble she'd been having at work and could have preempted this nightmare? He knew he would never know for sure, but he also knew the question would plague him for a very long time.

Somehow, Holly had known the battle he'd been waging about the decision he'd made. The woman who filled his soul with love and joy had instinctively sensed his turmoil. When he'd asked how she knew, she'd simply replied that it was her job to *know* what he needed as much as it was his to care for her.

Holly amazed him on so many levels, and if he lived to be a hundred, he was certain there wouldn't be a day go by when he didn't discover something new and wonderful about her. In a flash of insight, he remembered the expressions he'd seen on Logan's and Kalen's faces when he'd met them on the road because it was the same one he saw reflected in the mirror every morning since Holly had become his and Gage's.

Their marriage and commitment ceremonies had been a bonus, that was certain, but the real change had occurred as soon as he'd realized she was *theirs*. Everything in Jace's life had changed between one breath and the next, just as it had for Kalen and Logan.

As he sat watching the paramedics trying to talk Abby into letting them get her out from her warm cocoon so they could assess her, he had to smile when she only tightened her hold on Logan. He could tell them they were wasting their breath, but he doubted they'd listen. It was Kalen who'd finally manage to convince them their efforts would be better served by moving Abby to the local hospital as quickly as possible rather than provoking her any further. There wasn't room for him to ride in the ambulance with her, so he'd told them he would be following in a few minutes. But before Logan climbed into the back of the ambulance, Jace leaned forward and kissed her scratched and muddy cheek.

"You're in good hands, Short Round. I know Kalen and Logan will take good care of you—but remember, I loved you first."

Chapter 5

ABBY WAS CONVINCED she would never be warm again. She hadn't realized how bone-deep the cold had been until she'd been safe in Kalen's arms, and when Logan had stepped up to open his coat to her, she hadn't been able to resist. Nothing had ever felt as good as peeling off her wet shirt and bra, so she could press her bare skin against Logan's warm chest. Abby had felt him stiffen ever so slightly when her frigid skin met his warmth, but to his credit, he hadn't said a word.

Kalen had gently removed her wet running shoes and socks. She'd heard a couple of snaps, then he'd pulled thick wool socks over her feet. Almost immediately, she felt heat start to penetrate the cold. She figured the socks contained some type of activated heat device soldiers used, and right now, she was very grateful they had brought along their little goodie-bag of tricks.

She knew they were walking, and she'd heard Logan say they were meeting Jace. She sent up a silent prayer of thanks for her big brother and his friends. Logan reminded her she was bare from the waist up, and she knew he was trying to keep her from going "spider monkey" on Jace.

Whenever Jace had returned to the ranch, Abby had always greeted him by launching herself into his waiting arms and wrapping her arms and legs around him. They'd teased about being a little spider monkey, and for some reason, that memory seemed even sweeter because she'd just done the same thing to the two men she'd been crushing on for years.

Hearing her brother's voice had settled the last of Abby's fears, and she hadn't been able to hold back the fresh wave of tears when he'd used the nickname he'd called her since she'd been a young girl. When Jace had seen her collapse in their yard after being exposed to penicillin, she'd started calling him Indy. She'd been a huge Indiana Jones fan at the time, so naming him after her movie hero had seemed only natural. He'd responded by calling her Short Round which had been the name of the small Asian boy who was a fan favorite in the first movie. He'd insisted it was fitting because she was short, fearless, and always around.

In the back of her mind, it registered that he'd been talking to their parents on the phone, then she just let everything surrounding her slip away. Now that she was getting warm, the adrenaline crash was swamping her, and she was tired of fighting the bone-crushing fatigue she'd holding at bay for several hours. She barely remembered the paramedics trying to convince her to let them check her over, but she'd just clung to Logan and refused to let go.

LOGAN KNEW THE instant Abby had finally given in to the after-effects of the fear and cold. He'd been grateful for Kalen's intervention when the paramedics had insisted on taking her. She'd clung to him as if her life had depended on it, and he'd been unwilling to force her out of his arms.

Jace had been on the phone with Alex Lamont at the time, and by the time he'd hung up, the most belligerent of the ambulance crew had gotten a phone call that leeched all the color from his ruddy rat-face, and he'd suddenly become much more accommodating. Logan had to suppress his laughter because it was apparent the pissant had been tag-teamed by Alex and Zach Lamont.

Having served with them when they were all SEALs, Logan knew exactly how formidable the Lamonts were individually—and together they were a Cat-5 hurricane and bulldozer, rolled into one. Kalen leaned over and brushed Abby's hair back from her face.

"She looks like a battered angel." Logan looked down at her face and was transfixed by the wonder that was Abigail Garrett. Even with the scratches and bruises showing up on her cheek—*whoever did this to her has just signed their own death warrant*—she was still the most breathtakingly beautiful woman Logan had ever known.

Logan and Kalen both watched as Abby's long, curled lashes fluttered, brushing over the dark circles under her eyes before slowly lifting to reveal the windows to her sweet soul. Her eyes were such a deep shade of mahogany, they ordinarily looked almost black.

"I found a feather, so I knew I'd be okay... that you'd come for me, eventually. Thank you for listening to her." When she fell back to sleep, Logan looked up at Kalen and knew his friend was as confused by her cryptic comment as he'd been.

Kalen considered her words for several seconds before shrugging. "Maybe Jace will know what she meant." He'd just spoken the words when they'd pulled to a stop and were quickly swept up in the whirlwind of the emergency room in the small rural health center.

During the time they were sitting in the family room, waiting as the harried staff finished up the paperwork releasing Abby into her brother's care, Logan remembered her softly muttered comment and asked Jace about it. Jace's eyes went wide for a second before he smiled.

"Our granny always told us that if you find a feather, it means your guardian angel is near—like a sign or a reminder. It actually surprises me a little she remembered that story because she was pretty young when Granny died.

"Thank you. On behalf of Abby, my parents, and myself, thank you from the bottom of my heart. I know there have been a lot of false alarms with her trackers, and it probably wasn't easy to decide to interrupt my first evening home because I'd been pretty adamant about not wanting to be disturbed, but I'm grateful as hell you did."

Logan could tell Kalen was holding back his own emotion because Jace was right. There had been many false alarms, and it would have been very easy for Kalen to have just stalled for a few hours. Maybe Abby had been right, perhaps Kalen had listened to the whispered words of her guardian angel.

Chapter 6

KALEN KEPT ABBY tucked securely under his arm as they drove back to Washington. There wasn't any reason to call in any more favors to fly the short distance now that they weren't working against the clock. They'd also decided it wasn't wise to file a flight plan which would have put Abby on the radar of whoever had taken her.

Jace had been working with the local authorities to try to trace the owners of the cabins that lined the narrow mountain road where they'd found Abby. Everyone had hoped there would be someone who stood out as an obvious connection to the Energy Consortium, but so far, there hadn't been any leads.

"Did you speak with Mitch about tagging her files on the server?" Kalen had been catching bits and pieces of Jace's conversations and knew everything she'd been working on was still secure. But that didn't mean someone hadn't tried to get in or wouldn't try once they figured out they'd stolen a worthless computer, and their kidnapped researcher had slipped through their fingers as well.

"Already done." Jace smiled before continuing, "It was nice to know the man who broke into the top levels of the Pentagon's system just to prove to their Department of Defense contact, General Franklin, he could do it, refused to tap into Garrett Oil's server without speaking to *both* of my dads personally. Hell, he set it up so you can bet your ass he knows the thing inside and out. Christ, I'm glad he's our friend and not an enemy."

Before Abby was wheeled into the room by a nurse, who looked like she'd worked at least twenty-four straight, the three of them had discussed how to best keep her safe. They'd agreed they needed to get Abby's input, but the bottom line was they would simply do whatever it took. A couple of things had already been taken "off the table," including Abby returning to her Houston condo or the Garrett family ranch. The family also owned a cabin in the Colorado Rockies, and since that was public record, she couldn't go there either.

For now, the safest place for her was Logan and Kalen's apartment at Club Isola which happened to be next to the one Jace shared with Holly and Gage. Kalen was relieved he and Logan were finally going to have Abby under their roof, but he hadn't wanted it to be because she was in danger. Sighing to himself, he wondered what exactly her abductors had planned for her.

The fact they hadn't bound her meant either they'd been pressed for time or they really hadn't wanted her injured. If they'd been concerned with making certain she was unharmed, why didn't they let her ride in the front of the vehicle? Why put her in the damned trunk? There was just so much about the whole situation that didn't make sense, and often, that meant you were dealing with amateurs—and the problem with amateurs was that they were so damned unpredictable which often made them even more dangerous.

Abby had given the local Sheriff as much information as she could about the vehicle, but no one was surprised her main concern had been getting away without being seen rather than trying to memorize the license plate number. She'd been frustrated with herself for not thinking of it, but the elderly sheriff had reminded her to stop judging herself by "that horse shit you see on the television."

They'd all laughed about the elderly law enforcement officer's words, but he'd been right. The public thinks they should behave like the actors in the shows they watch, and it's almost always a set-up to fail situation. Kalen had seen it many times—victims being judged because they didn't think with a clear head. Of course, they weren't thinking clearly, they were fighting for their lives.

Kalen made a conscious effort to shake off that train of thought—anytime he considered what Abby had been going through and where her head must have been while she was running through the woods in the dark, it made him insane. Even without the rain, Abby hadn't been dressed warmly enough to spend the night in the mountains without proper shelter. The hospital staff had let her shower and given her clothing to wear, but her feet were so small, they didn't have any shoes to fit her. It hadn't mattered because he and Logan had been more than happy to have an excuse to carry her. Holding her in their arms would never be a hardship.

They had been amazed she hadn't even stirred when they boarded Ian's boat to cross over to the small island that housed Club Isola and the new resort. Ian and Callie also lived in a beautiful home on the western edge of the island. They were nearing completion on the "baby suite," which was a polite term for the addition they'd built so there would be a lot of traffic on and off the island in just a couple of hours. Hoping to avoid any of those workers seeing them bring Abby onto the island, they had skipped stopping to eat. Getting Abby safely inside the apartment wing of the club while they still had some cover of darkness would go a long way toward keeping her presence a secret for at least a day or two.

"Have you thought about how you are going to answer her questions about how we found her? Because they're coming, you know." Kalen had settled Abby on Logan's lap in the small parlor and had joined Jace at the bow.

"No fucking clue, but you're right, it's coming. Hell, all I can do is level with her. You and Logan are off the hook because you weren't here when we made the decision."

"But we've both known about it and haven't told her, so I doubt we'll just get a pass." Kalen didn't believe she would hold it against them, but he wanted to be prepared. "She's brilliant, but her sense of self-preservation needs a lot of work. We want her, Jace, and not just for a short fling. Logan and I have both wanted her for longer than you'll want to hear about, but we waited until she was old enough to make an informed decision about our lifestyle." Kalen ran his hand through black hair that was probably well past needing to be cut.

"I know your dads are both Doms, and your mom is their submissive, but I don't know how much Abby knows about their lifestyle since she was so young when she left for college. Although frankly, I can't imagine she has ever missed even the most subtle nuance—well, unless she was working and then she might have missed chainsaw-wielding masked men streaking through their damned living room." They both laughed, but Kalen sensed there was something his friend was holding back.

"If you know anything that will help us keep Abigail safe, please share it. You know her safety and happiness will always be our number one priority. Knowing what a tireless researcher she is, I doubt she is completely in the dark about the lifestyle."

I'm willing to bet she has looked at every major website available on the topic and probably has more explicit knowledge than many long-term submissives. I hope like hell she doesn't simply want to do one of her glorified empirical studies on the subject.

"Before you ask—yes, we plan to train her as our sub, but she has too much to contribute to the world for us to keep her at home barefoot and pregnant." Jace leaned his head back and laughed out loud at Kalen's last statement.

"Yeah, well, it would have been damned fun to watch you try. Christ, she'd skewer you if she even heard *that* mentioned. But all kidding aside, you are right, she does have a lot to contribute. Hell, her work on energy will revolutionize the industry if it goes the way it looks like it's going to go. She'll probably have a Nobel Prize before she's thirty, and anytime you rack up that much notoriety with research which will change the way trillion-dollar business-es operate, you are going to step on some toes."

Jace ran his hand through his hair, and Kalen knew his friend was getting close to the end of his patience. It had been a grueling few hours, and they were all skating on thin ice as far as their control was concerned.

"I refuse to apologize for the third tracker because it saved her life. She may be pissed, but she'll listen to reason, and if all else fails, I'll sick Ian on her. She idolizes him because he's as damned smart as she is. Hell, he personally funded her first lab." Jace chuckled and shook his head. For a few minutes, Kalen wasn't sure he was going to finish the story.

"She was thirteen, and we were talking over one of

Ian's earlier versions of a video phone call program. When he overheard her bemoaning the fact our parents wouldn't hand over ten grand so she could set up a lab in the basement, Ian hacked into her computer and had everything on her "wish list" delivered within the week. When she called to thank him, he admonished her to stop leaving her laptop online when it didn't need to be and told her she had to install the security programs he'd sent her before she set up any of the other equipment, then told her to 'change the world' before he'd ended the call."

"Jesus, who sends a thirteen-year-old ten thousand dollars in lab equipment?"

"Ian McGregor—because he believed in her. He still has a major financial stake in whatever she's working on. They are close. Very close. She considers him a mentor and another brother, much like Gage. Ian is very protective of her as well, so heads up to that. The thing is, I don't know how much sexual experience Abby has had. If I had to guess, I'd say little or none." Kalen knew his eyes must have conveyed his surprise.

"Yeah, I know—that's why I'm mentioning it. Be careful with her, she needs to understand tenderness before she can appreciate discipline. And I know how you and Boomer operate, you're both balls-to-the-wall with subs, so I just want you to understand exactly what you're getting into. And remember, I know where you fuckers live. Hurt her, and you die."

Kalen was wise enough to know even though the threat had been veiled in humor, Jace hadn't been kidding about not hurting Abby. What Jace didn't know was it was much more likely she would end up hurting the two of them.

Chapter 7

A BBY KNEW WHERE she was immediately even though the beautiful apartment Logan was carrying her through was a mirror image of Jace and Gage's. This one was decorated in a much more minimalist fashion, and the effect gave it an almost Zen-like feel. Knowing Kalen's interest in all things ancient and mystic, it was obvious he'd had the most input. When Logan didn't set her down but continued walking until they were in the master bath, Abby's eyes went immediately to the biggest walk-in shower she'd ever seen. There were two walls of black and silver tile and a third wall made up entirely of glass blocks.

Watching as Kalen started the water, Abby smiled when she saw they had shower heads at various heights on two walls in addition to several in the ceiling, but it was the lighting in the glass wall that really captured her interest. The lights seemed to be synched to the music playing from hidden speakers, and the effect was mesmerizing. Abby was so enthralled with the shower, she hadn't even noticed they both stripped and were almost finished removing her clothes as well.

"Step out, baby." Logan was kneeling at her feet, and she slowly lifted each leg so he could remove the draw-string pants the nurses had given her. He rose slowly, and when his mouth was even with her bare breast, his tongue snaked out and circled her nipple before he blew a puff of air over each one, smiling as they tightened into sharp points.

"Gorgeous. I can hardly wait to clamp these beauties. Your birthstone is ruby, right?" His teeth were putting just enough pressure on one of her stiff nipples, the pain was shooting electric bolts of pleasure straight to her sex. She felt her pussy flood with cream and hoped they moved her into the shower quickly before one of them noticed her juices were already coating the insides of her thighs.

Kalen was standing off to her right, leaning against the glass wall in a pose that should have looked casual but was anything but. He studied her with intent, and the hunger was plain to see.

"Abigail, I believe Logan asked you a question. You need to answer our questions immediately and with complete honesty. Keep in mind, love, editing your response or omitting information is still lying. Since we haven't talked about the rules yet, you're going to get a pass on that one, but for future reference, if we have to repeat a question or order, you'll be racking up punishments rather quickly."

"Punishments?" As soon as the word left her mouth, Abby realized she still hadn't answered the question Logan asked her. "Yes, the ruby is my birthstone." After their poolside interlude a few weeks ago, Abby had spent hours on the internet reading everything she could find about Dominance and submission. She'd even found a site that offered an interactive quiz designed to identify whether a person was a Dominant or submissive. Answering the questions had confirmed what she'd already known but didn't really understand because no one who knew her would ever describe her as submissive. When she'd chatted online with a few people who were associated with higher-end clubs like Club Isola and The ShadowDance Club, they'd explained being a sub and being a professional woman were not in any way at odds.

She'd talked to a woman in New York who had been in a Master/slave arrangement for over two decades, and she was also the head pediatric surgeon at one of the largest hospitals on the east coast. Abby had been relieved and thrilled to hear she didn't have to give up her life's work just to be in a D/s relationship even though she didn't understand the logistics of the relationships. Several of the subs she'd talked to assured her that as the submissive, she really had all the power. They taught her all about negotiating hard and soft limits, boundaries, safe words, and too many other things for her to even think about right now. When she refocused on Kalen, she saw his lips tilt up ever so subtly.

"Have a nice time on your little mental field trip, love?" Never one to hide behind feigned shyness, Abby plunged forward honestly.

"I was thinking about the research I did about Doms and subs." When Kalen just continued studying her, she went on, "I chatted online with a few of the subs who had been willing to answer my questions, and they told me there are a lot of professional women who are submissives outside of their careers, and they answered most of my questions, and well, I know I'm rambling, and you didn't really ask me anything except if I had a good time, so I guess I should just say that it was more of a brief refresher seminar than an actual field trip."

Well, snap. Could you sound any more like an academic, Abby? Maybe when catfish learn to do cartwheels, you'll learn when to shut up.

Abby's first clue she'd just spoken her thoughts out loud was Logan's failed attempt to smother his snort of laughter. Kalen's raised eyebrow was another pretty big clue. *Frack*.

"Catfish do cartwheels? Very interesting, but we don't mind if you sound academic, love. You *are* an academic, Abigail. Don't ever hide who you are—from us or anyone else."

Even though his words had sounded stern, Abby didn't miss the affection woven through them or how they warmed her heart.

"We want you Abigail, and we think you want us too, but we need to hear you say it. We have a lot to discuss, and it begins right now."

Abby felt a wave of pure need wash through her in a flash of heat that made her wonder if her skin was glowing. Both men now stood in front of her with their feet planted shoulder-width apart, their bulging biceps crossed over bare chests of rippled muscles she wanted to taste almost as much as she wanted her next breath.

"Yes, I want you, but I don't…well, I don't have much experience… but you probably already guessed that." She tried to keep her eyes on theirs, but it was just too much. It didn't matter that she'd slept during most of the trip back from the mountains, she was still emotionally drained, and that was always the worst time for her to make decisions. The irony was, right now, Abby wasn't sure she'd ever be able to back away from something her heart desired so much.

When they both reached for her hands, Abby followed them silently into the shower and stood quietly with her head tipped back and let the water flow over her face. The warm pulses of water relaxed her even more, and she considered for a minute that she should probably sit down, just as her knees buckled.

"Whoa, baby. Let's get you finished up and into bed." Logan had caught her before she'd gone clear to the floor, and he held her against his chest while Kalen washed and conditioned her long hair. She quickly found herself lost in the moment. The feel of Kalen's hands massaging her scalp and the feeling of Logan's light dusting of chest hair scraping against her breasts caused Abby to arch and tilt her head further back as she moaned at the sensations bombarding her.

"Fuck me. Baby, you need to stop unless you're up to water sports because you are playing with fire here."

"Please..." Abby wasn't even sure what she was begging for, all she knew was her body was filled with a deep need only these two men could fill. She closed her eyes against the water raining down from the overhead showerheads, but when both men went completely still, she brought her head back up and opened her eyes. She was suddenly cold again, but this time it was because of the rejection she was sure was in their expressions. She looked but didn't really make any effort to *see*... she just tried to quickly step to the side so she would be out from between them.

"*Stop.*" Kalen's voice stopped her immediately, but she didn't look up. "Look at us, Abigail." She slowly raised her face, making sure she had masked the hurt she felt before she faced them. "Tell us why you tried to leave. What went through that brilliant mind of yours that could have possibly been so inaccurate?"

What? Did he just say inaccurate? Abby looked closely and was surprised to see their lust-filled faces watching her intently.

"You stopped moving when I, well... when I said please, and I just couldn't take another rejection. I mean it's been a long time and everything, but I still remember how it felt, and then you didn't finish that day by the pool, so I figured maybe I had it wrong. Maybe you want me but don't really *want me*... you know what I mean?" She hadn't meant to spit all of that out in one breath, but at least it was done.

Abby knew she was intellectually gifted, but she also knew her social skills had taken a big hit because she'd been so focused on getting through school, then she'd poured all of her energy into her research. She hadn't had all the same exposure to dating and the opposite sex in general as other women her age. Hell, it wasn't like the "college scene" had been open and welcoming to a sixteen-year-old girl. She'd simply gone to classes, then back to the small apartment her parents had rented for her. The residents of the building had quickly adopted her, and even the doormen knew her schedule and had her cell phone number on speed dial.

Abby had stopped for supplies one day without letting building security know and had gotten three phone calls within fifteen minutes, not including the calls she'd gotten from both of her dads. She still remembered that day vividly because she'd been both pleased and annoyed at the attention that short delay had drawn.

Later that evening, she'd gotten a call from Ian McGregor. He'd told her about the bracelet he was having delivered to her. At that time, it was a prototype and linked to his cell phone as well as the newly formed security team in Colorado. It had been a couple of years before she'd found out she was being monitored by the staff of one of the country's most exclusive and popular BDSM clubs.

While Jace had been in the SEALs, Ian had kept up-grading her bracelets and had often delivered them himself. Her friends had always clamored to meet the handsome billionaire she had always considered another big brother of sorts.

When she had started working on the politically controversial biofuels project for Garrett Oil, Jace had already retired from the SEALs and taken over Ian's security team. Her brother had wanted to add an additional level of security, but she'd fought him tooth and nail. It had only been when Ian had flown to Houston and pled their case, she finally conceded their concerns might have some validity, but her abductors had taken her backpack and all of her jewelry so...

KALEN WATCHED ABBY and could almost hear the well-oiled wheels of her mind spinning. When she'd rattled off some nonsense about not really wanting her, he hadn't had the faintest idea what she'd meant even though she'd assumed they had. When he'd looked up at Logan, it had been clear he didn't understand her remark either. Before they could respond, she'd gone off into her own head, and he'd instinctively known where it was going to end. It was only a matter of seconds until he saw the questions dance through her expressions, and then...yep, there it was, the moment she realized the trackers had been missing, and they'd found her, anyway.

Abby took a step back, and the look of distrust and vulnerability suddenly filling her eyes was gut-wrenching to watch. The eyes that had been filled with passion just a few short minutes ago were now overflowing with questions and insecurity. When she tried to cover herself from their view, he'd had enough.

"Don't. Don't ever cover yourself from our view, Abigail. I'm sure I speak for Logan as well when I tell you I don't, in fact, have any idea what you mean by 'want you but not really wanting you.' That is about a hundred and eighty degrees out, love. We have wanted you for a very long time, but we were waiting until you were ready."

She had dropped her hands to her sides, but her expression held none of the heat it had earlier, and for the first time in his adult life, Kalen was at a total loss how to proceed. He took a deep breath and ran his hand through his hair, hoping the extra few seconds would provide the gods time to infuse him with some kind of insight—they didn't. *Evidently, everyone in the mystic realm is on a fucking break.*

Chapter 8

L OGAN HAD BEEN listening to Abby's thoughts or at least the bits and pieces he could pick up. He wasn't as gifted as Mitch, but Logan had been an empath as long as he could remember. Until Callie McGregor, he'd only been able to pick up another person's emotions if he was touching them, and the emotions were strong enough.

Callie had been the first person he'd actually been able to "read" as Mitch called it. Logan had argued it was actually "hearing," but Mitch had just shrugged him off. Mitch had also been helping him fine-tune his skill, and right now, he was very grateful for the time they'd spent on video calls, working together.

Mitch had warned him that listening to Abby was always going to be a challenge because her mind worked at such a high level of processing and so fast, her thoughts would be hard to track. Logan was grateful she'd actually spoken some of it aloud, so he'd been able to fill in a few of the blanks. He'd seen the frustration in Kalen's face and had almost felt sorry for the man—it was obvious that, for the first time, the Dom who was so well known in BDSM circles as controlled and insightful was at a complete loss with Abby. Logan understood because when the stakes are higher, the fear of misstep was more intense—and the stakes with this particular woman couldn't possibly be any higher. Logan studied her closely, waiting for the right moment to speak up.

"Ask your question, baby. We'll never lie to you. There may be times we can't tell you everything for various security reasons, but if that happens, we'll tell you straight up."

There were several seconds where the only sounds were those made by the falling water and the music surrounding them before he saw the moment when he knew she was ready. *Oh yeah, here it comes, chin tilted up, shoulders back, and eyes focused. Yes indeed, both barrels pointed right this way. Fuck.*

"How did you know? Both of my trackers were gone. How did you find me so fast?" Logan nodded once, so she knew her question was understood and valid.

"There is a third tracker. One Jace and Ian considered a sort of 'panic alarm.' It is *only used* if the other two go off-line, and even then, only Jace or Ian can authorize its activation. Before you ask—yes, Kalen and I both knew about it, but only after the fact, so we weren't in on the decision to implement it." When he saw the fire rage in her eyes he smiled, "Baby, we might not have been here when it happened, but we'd have backed them. I know you aren't happy, but stop for just a minute and think about how differently everything would have ended yesterday without their foresight." Both of her eyes filled with tears and resignation.

"Well, horseshoes and hand-grenades. How am I supposed to be pissed about this now? Frack, this just plain sucks, I tell ya. I really have every right to be mad at those two buffoons. I mean seriously… this is huge. That's why my leg got so warm, isn't it? Of course, it is. This is why Ian was so involved in my medical care after my skiing accident. Geez, I handed them the opportunity on a damned silver platter, boy, that frosts my cookies. Damn, I hate enabling their techno-stalking bullshit. Boy oh boy, my brother is in deep this time. I like Holly, but she may have to do with half the nookie for a while."

Logan let out a breath he hadn't even known he was holding and smiled at her tirade. Her brother and Ian were going to get an earful, but it was obvious she'd already moved past the worst of the storm that had been clouding her thoughts.

"Well, you will have to take that up with the two of them, but right now Kalen and I have other plans for you, baby. Before we start, let's get a couple of things out of the way. First of all, are you on any sort of birth control?"

"Yes." Her eyes went wide, and heat was returning to their chocolate depths... and that was all that mattered. When he simply raised a brow at her cryptic answer she shrugged. "My periods were crazy intense and with my travel schedule... well, you get the idea." He had three older sisters, so he was pretty sure he knew exactly what she was talking about, and it wasn't all timing. "And I'm clean, I have a report in my pur... oh, well, I guess I don't have a copy of it, but I haven't had sex since my last checkup."

Well, that was interesting. She'd been looking right at both of them until that last statement, then her eyes had dropped straight to the floor. Well, not directly to the floor, her gaze had locked on to both of their cocks for the briefest of moments before she realized they were watching her check them out. The little imp hadn't lied to them, he knew that much, but there was certainly something she wasn't sharing. Decided to wait and see how things went before pushing her, he went on.

"We are both clean and have reports if you'd like to see them. We don't want anything between us, baby. When we slide into your sweet body, we want to feel every glorious bit of wetness and each ripple of your channel as you rock our worlds."

Logan watched her eyes dilate, and the pulse at the base of her neck speed up as her arousal regained its lost ground. As if they'd choreographed it in advance, he and Kalen moved at the exact same moment. Logan quickly took his own shower while Kalen silenced Abby's protests and soaped her from head to toe.

THE FEEL OF Kalen's callused hands gliding over every inch of her soapy body was so sensual, Abby was worried she'd come from it alone. She hadn't even realized she was moaning until she heard Kalen's chuckle.

"Do you like the feel of my hands mapping your perfect body, love?"

Wonder what gave me away? The moaning or swooning?

"Yes. It is like being massaged with living, breathing, wet silk. The touch is electrical and magnetic, and the combination is almost too much to take in." She wondered about her inability to accurately describe what she was feeling. *Damn Abby, you get naked and wet, and your brain turns to mush, and your vocabulary reverts to fifth grade. What the hell is wrong with you?*

Abby knew Kalen was standing behind her, and it struck her as odd because of the extreme differences in height, and she couldn't help the giggle that escaped her lips. Knowing her reaction had been totally inappropriate, considering she had just confessed to being over the top aroused by his touch, she leaned her head back.

"I'm sorry, that was rude. It's just that you are both so tall and with you standing directly behind me like that… well, your cock is so hard, and I can feel it against my back and… *oh my God in heaven…*" Kalen stepped back and delivered two sharp swats to each of her ass cheeks, and the pain had barely registered before it blossomed into lightning streaks of pure pleasure-driven desire.

"We are going to have to talk to our friends who have intelligent subs and learn some of their tricks for silencing their minds, Boomer." Even though Kalen's words had been directed at Logan, Abby had no doubt they were really for her ears. She wanted to tell them both she wished them luck because she'd been trying for years to figure out how to do that very thing, and quite frankly, it was exhausting. Her mind had a loud voice and was rarely quiet, for any reason. The closest she ever came to what she called mind-silence was that point in a workout when you are just minutes away from collapsing in exhaustion. Invariably, by the time she undressed for a shower, the chatter was back on, and it usually seemed like it was trying to make up for lost time. Sighing inwardly, Abby couldn't help but wonder if there really was a way to set it all aside.

KALEN WASN'T SURE he'd ever met anyone who could check in and out so easily. Hell, if he didn't already know Abby as well as he did, he might not even realize she was slipping in and out of the moment. She'd obviously learned some damned effective coping skills, but they'd teach her more. When he looked up at Logan, his friend was shaking his head in obvious amusement and wonder.

"Unbelievable. If I didn't know how fucking brilliant she is, I'd be pissed we aren't holding her interest. Christ, I've heard Alex and Zach mention this, and I know it is an ongoing challenge for Ian, but I had no idea..." Kalen wanted to laugh at Logan's blunt assessment but couldn't find a single flaw in his view.

Kalen moved Abby to where Logan was waiting with a large towel. He quickly finished up his own shower, then joined them. When she seemed to be looking for something, he helped her smooth on the body lotion she asked for. Logan combed through her tangled hair as Abby watched him curiously. When she thanked him and asked where he'd acquired that particular skill, Kalen saw the vulnerability of a woman worrying about her predecessors, and insecurity shone in her pretty eyes. As an experienced Dom, Logan hadn't missed the look either.

"I have three older sisters, baby, and they all had very long hair I often helped them with in exchange for them making my favorite treats. Contrary to Mr. Healthy over there," he nodded to Kalen, "I will do most anything for a plate of warm snickerdoodle cookies."

Abby's expression immediately cleared, and her eyes danced. "I'll keep that in mind and make you some should you ever need your smoke detector checked to see if it's functioning properly." Kalen snorted a laugh because he remembered Jace telling them several Abby *vs* "The Kitchen" tales, including one that had her parents begging the owners of the apartment building she lived in during grad school to not evict her after she'd had several late-night visits from the local fire department.

Jace had told them Abby was much too *distracted* to even be trusted to boil water. Evidently, the time she'd tried to hard boil eggs for Easter had become something of a family legend. The night they heard that particular story, they'd all been sitting around the fire in her parents' backyard when Jace had told them the details with great embellishment, most likely. Abby had simply shrugged and said she'd been "set-up" because her mother had secretly wanted to remodel the kitchen.

Chapter 9

LOGAN SPUN ABBY around in his arms and easily lifted her up onto the bathroom's long vanity and stepped between her legs. He smiled at her small gasp when her warm, bare ass connected with the cool marble.

"Baby, we aren't the least bit interested in your cooking ability, I assure you. We'll happily cook for you, so you don't cause any major disasters. My guess is Ian and Jace are already drawing up some memo that forbids you from even trying." He pressed his finger against her lips when he saw her open her mouth to respond.

"Before you say anything, remember this apartment is wired for sight and sound. For privacy reasons, most of the rooms require a code for access, but there *are* several people with those codes, and the kitchen is fair game for any of the security staff to view." He fought back the smile that threatened to surface as he heard her thinking if they had "hot kitchen sex" people might be able to see.

Well, well, seems our little subbie might be a bit of an exhibitionist. How interesting.

Logan used his hands to tilt her head slightly before pressing his lips to hers. Tracing the line where her lips met with his tongue, he surged through as soon as she opened to him. The kiss went straight to plundering in seconds. Logan moved his hands to her breasts and pinched both nipples hard enough to cause her to gasp.

"When I clamp these, you're going to feel the pleasure/pain wash over you in crashing waves of ecstasy, baby." Lowering his right hand, he rotated his wrist and slid a finger just inside her and stilled.

He and Kalen had known it was likely Abby was inexperienced, but he certainly hadn't expected this. The barrier his finger came up against was both a thrilling gift and a terrifying responsibility. When he didn't move, he didn't *hear* but *felt* the wave of panic that filled Abby. Removing his hand from her sex, he wrapped his arms around her and pulled her small frame into his arms. Christ, he could wrap his arms around her and still touch his fingertips to his opposing shoulders.

He and Kalen were going to have to be careful they didn't injure her in the course of regular BDSM play, they were so much larger than she was. The idea they might hurt Abby in any way brought him up short, and he nearly shuddered at the thought. When Logan looked up, Kalen was looking at him, concern etching itself in the fine lines bracketing his friend's eyes. Making sure Abby couldn't see him in the mirror, he mouthed the word *virgin* and saw Kalen's eyes go from shock to blazing in a heartbeat.

"Abby, this is the most incredible gift you could ever give us. To be your first and know we have the opportunity to make the memory perfect for you—well, baby, there just aren't any words to tell you how honored we are by this gift. I can feel the tension in your body and know you misread my reaction to what I found. Now, enough talking, Kalen and I want to play with you before we claim you as our own."

Logan was grateful he'd dropped his towel in the hamper before picking Abby up when she wrapped her legs around him and pressed her wet heat against the spongy head of his erect cock. Just the feeling of her slick folds rolling over the hypersensitive tip caused his breath to hitch.

"Fuck me, baby. Your pussy is so wet and hot, I can't wait to slide inside of you." Logan and Kalen had shared women for years and had known almost from the beginning that they wanted a polyamorous marriage. But never in all of those years had Logan ever been more grateful for their team efforts because right now, his desire for Abby was so great, he wasn't sure he'd be able to properly prepare her for his penetration without Kalen's help.

Every instinct in him was screaming *take, possess, claim,* and fighting off the burning need pulsing through him to push as deep as he could was surely going to be an epic battle. Making tonight a memory Abby would cherish for the next fifty or sixty years *had* to take precedence.

Chapter 10

K ALEN HAD BEEN momentarily stunned by Logan's *discovery*, but his next breath was accompanied by a flash of desire so hot and intense, it blindsided him. Jace had warned him Abby was probably inexperienced, but Kalen doubted her brother had any idea she was completely innocent. Something in the back of Kalen's mind questioned how a brilliant and beautiful woman had flown below the radar of the entire male population, but he'd never been one to question the fates, so he let the question slide from his mind.

Settling alongside Abby on the huge bed they'd had built for the master bedroom, Kalen bent his elbow and propped his head in his hand so he could look at the beautiful woman lying between him and Logan. They'd waited for her for so long, the moment felt a bit surreal. Having her naked and spread out so gloriously between them was a dream come true.

There wasn't any question about who would take her first. Logan was a bit longer than Kalen, but Kalen's cock was broader. They'd both heard from numerous subs they'd done scenes with over the years, their sizes had worried them at first. He'd always been grateful for the women who'd spoken openly during their aftercare. He and Logan had made changes in the way they worked together on several occasions based on feedback they'd gotten from those open-minded submissives.

"You are a wonder, love. There is an echo of your Native American heritage in every breath you take, and the spirits of your ancestors dance around you. It's in the energy that surrounds you, and it is an amazing feeling just to be near you." Kalen meant each and every word he spoke to her.

He had always been drawn to the mystical spirit inside Abigail Garrett, he felt it call to him from the first moment he'd met her, and it hadn't mattered she was just a young girl at the time, that immediate *pull* had been purely spiritual rather than physical. Kalen had always thought Abby was an old soul, and as she'd matured, it had become obvious he'd been right. Abby's ability to see a better future and learn from the mistakes of those who had passed before her had always been one of the things he found the most intriguing.

Every member of their team who visited the Garrett Ranch commented on how Abby's mind was never still. More than once, he and the others had deliberately engaged her in several different conversations simultaneously about totally unrelated topics just to see how long she could keep up, and she'd never missed a beat. Hell, several of them had become so confused, the whole thing had ended up sounding like an Abbott and Costello routine.

Abby and Jace's fathers had been standing just outside the ring of seats surrounding the outdoor fire pit, shaking their heads and laughing. The oldest of the family patriarchs, William Garrett, had told Kalen a few days later, they'd gotten wind of the plan and had come outside to watch Abby talk circles around the Special Forces hotshots his son regularly brought home.

"You boys are playin' outta your league. Abby's not just gifted intellectually, you know. The angels love her, they danced the day she was born. I swear on the souls of my ancestors, I saw them in her mama's room. Wes and I have always known how special she is, and I don't want you or Logan to ever forget we know—get my drift?"

Kalen had indeed known exactly what the man was telling him, but he'd been blown away they'd recognized his and Logan's attraction to their daughter even before they had allowed it to fully gel in their own minds. When he'd nodded and assured her father she would always be safe with them, the man had nodded and replied, "I believe she will be at that." He'd turned to his brother and smiled. "Our work here is done. Let's go find Pilar and let her remind us why we both worship the ground she walks on." The two had laughed and walked back to the house, and Kalen had seen himself and Logan in them for just a moment before the image faded.

Shaking off the memory, Kalen watched Logan move into position between Abby's toned legs. When Logan smiled up at her and told her not to come until one of them gave her permission, Kalen heard her sharp intake of breath.

"If you will put yourself in our care and follow our instructions, we'll send you into orbit several times before we take you, so your body is as ready as it can be, love." Abby turned to look at him, and her smile lit a fire deep in his soul.

"I trust you. I trust you both, and I want you so much, it scares me because it has been my experience if I want something desperately, fate likes to play hide and seek with it." Kalen had never heard it stated in exactly that way, but her words rang with truth for him as well. But this time, he and Logan would see to it they delivered on their promises and fate would just have to catch a ride on the next train.

"Not this time, love. This is a moment in time we have all been waiting for. Now, not another word unless you are frightened or hurting. You won't need a safe word tonight because this is us making love to the woman who captured our attention years ago. Tonight is about making a memory we'll all hold close to our hearts forever. In the future, we'll expect you to say yellow if you are getting close to being overwhelmed and need to take a break or ask a question. Later, we'll remind you if you say red, everything stops." He brushed the dark silk strands of her hair back from her face and smiled at her. "Tonight is about us introducing you to pleasure, so no more words unless we ask you a question or you are struggling, do you understand?" He'd laced his last sentence with just enough of his Dom tone, he knew she would instinctively understand it had been more of an order than a question, and he knew she had indeed understood when she nodded her understanding.

In his peripheral vision, Kalen saw Logan lower his mouth to her waxed sex, watching Abby's eyes widen, then dilate fully as pleasure played over her face like a beautiful marquee advertising lust and arousal. The visual had him shifting uncomfortably, trying to relieve some of the pressure threatening to have him spilling before he'd even really gotten to touch her.

LOGAN LICKED ABBY from her rear rosette all the way up

until he could circle her clit and coax it out from under its hood. Abby was so responsive—a fine musical instrument that was a siren's call to the artistry of a well-trained Dom. He and Kalen had been Doms most of their adult lives, so they were certainly attuned to each and every one of her responses—no matter how subtle. Feeling the muscles in her thighs twitch as he took her higher and higher up the mountain, he knew she was quickly coming upon the point of no return, so he backed off just a bit and was rewarded by a soft moan of protest.

"Soon, baby. I want you to soar over the moon, so let me make sure you are well prepared for the trip." Refocusing his attention on her sex, he slid his arms under her knees and lifted them up and out, so she was completely exposed to him. "You are so beautiful. Your pussy is a rich, dark rose color, and the folds are engorged with blood, making them look like a rose in full bloom."

Tracing the folds with his tongue in slow sweeping motions was pushing her limits, and he knew he needed to move on before she built an orgasm that would shatter her and prevent her from being capable of enjoying the rest of the pleasures they had planned. He stiffened his tongue and began thrusting it just inside her vagina in a preview of what was to come. When he felt her muscles twitching rapidly, he locked eyes with Kalen and blinked once, giving his friend the okay. Kalen had been painting her tight, pink nipples with his tongue but pulled back and moved to lick the shell of her tiny ear as he whispered, "Come for us, Abigail."

Logan was surprised at the immediacy of her response. It was a testament to the speed at which her mind processed information and the strength of their connection. She was coming before Kalen had even spoken her name.

Logan was grateful he'd already encircled her thighs with his arms, or she would have arched right out of his hold. Her scream had likely triggered the sound and motion-activated cameras in the hallway. Holly had done the same thing not long ago when her men had taken her in their kitchen. Jace and Gage had claimed bragging rights about the incident for several days.

Before Abby had even finished with her climax, Logan moved into position and slid up against the barrier. "Are you ready, baby? I'm sorry, I know this is going to hurt you, but I promise you it will be worth it." She was still catching her breath, and her eyes were beautifully glazed with passion, but she found enough focus to nod, and he pushed through in a quick stroke. This time her scream sounded entirely different, and it broke his heart.

He could feel the warmth of the blood and wondered, for just a moment, if he should check and make sure she wasn't bleeding too much. Before he could pull back, she surprised him by wrapping her legs around his waist and pressing herself against him in a thrust of her hips and pull of her legs that pushed the tip of his cock up against the opening of her womb in the time it took him to blink.

"*Fuck!* Oh, my fucking God, Abby. I cannot believe you did that. Christ, woman, I—oh my God, you feel unbelievable. Your sweet little cunt is squeezing me like a fist, and I can barely catch my breath. Resisting the urge to pound into you is getting harder by the second. Stop moving baby, or this is going to be hard, fast, and over before you are ready to come with me." He was grateful she seemed to be at least trying to still the flexing of her vaginal wall muscles.

Logan could count on one hand the number of times he'd failed to anticipate a sub's movement, but Abby hadn't given him any clue, and he suspected that it hadn't been planned on her part, rather it had been some kind of instinctual response, but he still planned to paddle her pert little ass for it. At the very least, she'd topped from the bottom by taking control of the situation, and even though they'd told her this wasn't a scene, she'd taken a huge risk with her safety. He couldn't and wouldn't ignore it.

THE PAIN ABBY had felt as Logan pushed through the membrane guarding her virginity had shocked her, and when he stopped moving, all she could think about was she hadn't taken that moment of agony for no reason. She damned well intended to get her money's worth out of it that was for sure. There was likely going to be hell to pay later for what she'd done, but damn, it had felt good to feel Logan slide into her pussy. She was sure he had stretched the walls of her channel to their max, and there had been a flash of heated pain that morphed into pleasure so quickly, she wasn't sure the pain hadn't been a figment of her imagination.

As her sensitive tissues stretched to accommodate him, she wondered for a moment if she was going to be able to take Kalen. Trying to let go of the worry, she looked up at Logan and saw him grin. He kissed her, then whispered in her ear, "He'll fit just fine. Don't worry, baby." Abby relaxed for just a few seconds before the slide of Logan's cock in and out of her sheath had her heart racing to the point she was starting to see spots in front of her eyes.

"Breathe, Abby." Logan's words were sharp, and she knew he'd used that tone to snap her mind back into gear.

"I'm going to paddle your ass until you can't even sit down for that little stunt, baby." She felt her pussy go liquid at his words, and she was mortified that her body had just snitched her out to the gorgeous Dom with his cock as deep inside her as he could possibly get.

"Well, well. Kalen, it seems our little subbie likes the idea of a paddling. She just soaked my cock with her sweet honey." He had been speaking to Kalen, but his eyes had never left hers, and it had felt like she was being electrified from the inside. "Tell me what you need, baby because all of a sudden, I'm getting the idea slow and sweet isn't gonna do it for ya, is that about right?"

Abby's heart almost melted because she knew he was stalling to give her body a chance to adjust to his size, but he was also giving her a choice, and from everything she'd read about Doms, that was not the way things usually went down. Even though Logan was holding her tightly in place, preventing her from tilting or thrusting her hips the way she wanted to, she could flex her internal muscles and caress him in the most intimate way she knew how.

"Jesus Christ, baby—that felt amazing. And while I do understand that answer, we'll always require you to answer our questions with words. Your answers need to be immediate, complete, and honest—always."

Abby felt the bed shift, and Kalen kissed her ear, his words a warm touch against her skin. "You better get your voice and brain to work in tandem quickly, love. If you are ready for Logan to fuck you like he wants to, you better answer his question, *right now*."

"Yes, please. I don't want slow and easy, I'm ready, and I've waited so long." Abby let the words tumble out in a rush before she had time to think about them, fearing if she applied logic, she might not be honest with them—or herself.

Logan's answering smile was a flash before he pulled out slowly, then pushed back in with more force than she had been expecting, and Abby caught the scream just before it passed her lips. She damned well didn't want him to think he'd hurt her and stop, and she was sliding over the edge quickly.

"Your body and soul both respond so beautifully, love. You have no idea how deeply that touches your Masters. Let it take you, Abigail. Surrender your mind to the needs of your body."

In some corner of her consciousness, Abby registered the word Masters, but she couldn't protest because there was a truth woven so tightly into the fabric of his words, she knew it was an argument she didn't want to win. Logan was pushing in and out of her with barely restrained thrusts that were hitting her G-spot, and she suddenly realized she was already screaming her release.

Abby felt as if she'd been blindsided by a pleasure so overwhelming, she couldn't wrap her head around it, and she hadn't even known she was close to coming. The entire world seemed to burst into sparkling colors, and the feeling of flying was the freest thing she'd ever experienced. She heard Logan's shout as he followed her into oblivion, but she really couldn't think about anything but the beauty of the place he'd just sent her to and how thrilling it had been to finally be able to shut out the voices that were always chattering in her head. Abby knew her heart was lost to both men, but Logan had been the first man to show her the bliss of that silence, and that was an even sweeter gift than making her first sexual experience so perfect.

Chapter 11

K ALEN HAD NEARLY come just from watching their woman's response to Logan. Ordinarily, a Dom wouldn't fuck a virgin the way Logan had just done with Abby, but she was far from ordinary. They hadn't intended to treat this as a scene, but Logan had known exactly what their sub had needed, and he'd given it to her in spades. Kalen handed Logan the warm cloth he'd gotten while the two of them had been trying to regain their bearings. He and Logan cringed when they saw the blood smearing her thighs. Kalen had never taken a woman's virginity, so he hadn't been prepared for that particular visual or how much it haunted him.

Logan left Abby in his care and went to clean himself. Kalen looked down at her and was surprised to see insecurity in her eyes. "Abigail? Talk to me, love. What's put that uncertainty in your beautiful eyes?" When she shifted slightly and tried to cover her naked body, he stopped her by simply placing his palm on her abdomen. "No hiding, Abigail. Talk. Now. Are you hurt?"

"No. I was just wondering why you aren't, I mean why you don't seem to want... frack." Her confusion would have amused him any other time because she was usually so self-assured, and he'd rarely seen her off her game in any way, but this was not a moment to tease her. It was too important and having her believe he didn't want her was absolutely unacceptable.

"Oh, Abigail, I assure you that I want you with every fiber, every cell, and every breath. I want your body to have a few minutes to talk to you because if I'd asked you immediately if you were too sore to take me, you would have still been swimming in endorphins, and those are great little painkillers so you might have said you were alright when you really aren't. Does that make sense?" Kalen saw her eyes widen in understanding, and she quickly nodded her head. "Now that you're back on a more even keel, what do you think? And, love, I want an honest answer, not one you think I want to hear."

"I am a bit sore, but not too sore." When she reached up and raked her fingers over his stubbled cheek and smiled, he was undone by his love for her. "I want you too, Kalen, and I think it's important you and I have this moment together. From everything I've learned, we need to start in the way we want our relationship to proceed. I know in Dom-speak it's 'begin as you intend to go' but from my side of things, it is equally important." In one move, Kalen rolled her to her back and positioned himself over her. Feeling his throbbing cock slide through her wet folds caused him to groan.

"You call to me in a way no other woman ever has, love. The magic of the universe swirls inside your soul." He flexed his hips just enough to move the head of his cock inside her heat. "*Fuck*, you are so hot and wet for me. I want to savor you like the sweet treat you are, but you are testing my control."

All his plans to take her slowly, making sweet love to her disintegrated when she rotated her hips just enough to let the tight outer ring of muscles at the opening of her channel rub over the sensitive skin at the base of the corona of his cock. That one movement was all it took, and Kalen started pushing in and out of her, gaining depth with each thrust. Each new inch he pushed into her heat brought another layer of desire until Kalen wasn't sure he'd survive.

Hearing Abby's soft sounds of pleasure sent his own arousal up so quickly, he was worried he was going to come before she found her own release, and that was absolutely not how this was supposed to go. Filling his mind with abstract concepts from his studies—different principles from obscure philosophers whose ideas were still studied despite the puzzling questions surrounding their significance—was barely enough to pull him back from the edge.

"You are stealing my control, love. The rippling of the inner walls of your sweet pussy tells me you are close, and I want to feel you come apart in my arms. Know that you are always safe with us. We want every part of you because you already own both of us—heart and soul. Come for me, Abigail." In less time than it took him to sink deep, she clamped down on him so tight, Kalen wasn't sure he would have been able to stroke her again. The rippling contractions of her walls were more powerful than the tightest fist and milked his seed from him. Feeling his cum splash against her cervix brought out an animalistic roar from deep within him he barely recognized. *No other woman— ever. She owns me, and she belongs to us.*

There hadn't been any question about whether he and Logan wanted Abby, but now he wasn't sure he would ever be able to live without her in his life. Kalen knew before they started working out exactly how the three of them could spend their lives together, they needed to make sure Abby was safe. The thought of someone harming her sent a shard of ice-cold fear straight through his heart.

With his mind racing and his body gasping for air, Kalen rolled to his side, so he didn't crush her under his weight. He didn't know how long he lay there with his cock still inside of her, but when he moved and felt their combined juices slide from her, he was filled with a primal sense of satisfaction he knew men had felt since the dawn of time. There was something very grounding about sharing an experience men through the ages have relished.

Taking the warm cloth from Logan, Kalen cleaned Abby carefully and was relieved to see there wasn't any blood. Even before he'd dried her, he could tell she'd fallen asleep. Logan's voice brought him back from his thoughts.

"She's even more than I'd ever dreamed she'd be, but we haven't gotten to the hard stuff yet. She's been essentially on her own since she was fifteen, and it's going to be a big adjustment for her to have two very Alpha Doms who want nothing more than to shield her from the world.

Kalen nodded in agreement but didn't add anything to his friend's remarks because quite frankly, he thought Logan had summed things up pretty well. By the time he returned from cleaning up, Logan had tucked the covers around Abby and dressed. Kalen quickly donned his own jeans, pulled on a t-shirt, and followed him out to the kitchen.

"I just called Jace and asked for an update. He and Gage are on their way over, and Ian will be here in just a few minutes." Kalen looked at his watch and was surprised to find out it was already early evening which meant he and Logan had been awake for almost forty-eight hours. Ordinarily, he didn't like to use caffeine as a crutch to stay awake, but he needed to be alert for this meeting. Keeping

Abby safe was much more important than his discomfort about relaxing his own rules. As he set the coffee pot to brew, he looked over at Logan and laughed at his friend's surprised expression.

"Don't even start. I'm running on fumes, and I think we both know this thing is probably not going to be as simple as it appears on the surface."

"I agree. My gut is screaming at me about this. Jace mentioned they'd already talked to the Lamonts, and they've agreed to help." Logan's words went a long way to settle Kalen's sense of foreboding because the Shadow-Dance team was second to none, and their connections were the stuff of any security team's dreams.

Before he could answer, the door opened and the room quickly filled with people, and for the first time, Kalen wasn't unnerved by having so many people in his private space because each and every one of them was here to help the woman who had just burned her name into his heart and stolen his soul.

Chapter 12

L OGAN HAD KNOWN the threats against Abby probably ran deeper than just some competitive bullshit related to her project's financial implications, but he'd been surprised at everything they'd learned during the meeting they hosted around at their small kitchen table. The first thing he'd asked was when Abby's presentation before the Senate committee would be. He knew it had been rescheduled after her abduction, but the news she was expected to present her findings the next morning shocked him. Ian had been the first one to address his concerns.

"It's a power game. The asshat demanding this take place so quickly has close ties to the current administration, and they are not at all happy Abby is still working for the private sector. Keep in mind, we are talking about billions of dollars in revenue from the patents alone, not money the powers that be are anxious to see slip through their fingers."

"Ian's right and there are some fairly significant rumors out there this snatch-and-grab might not have been the work of the Consortium although they certainly aren't above it." Jace didn't look convinced, but the bottom line was they didn't know who was responsible. "When you consider one of the cabins at the end of the road Abby's kidnappers were traveling is used as a safe-house for various alphabet agencies, including all our local spooks, the evidence starts to look pretty daunting."

"Have you guys asked her what she remembers, or were you too focused on assuring yourselves she was alive and well?" Alex and Zach Lamont were joining them via video conferencing, and Zach addressed his question to Kalen and Logan. His tone had been teasing, and Kalen appreciated his effort to lighten their mood. The irony was Zach was absolutely right, neither of them had even thought to ask Abby any questions, and Logan was actually a bit stunned at that realization, but he was even more surprised to hear Abby's sweet voice behind him.

"Hi, Zach, and does Kat know you've gotten to be so ornery?"

Zach Lamont leaned his head back and roared out his laughter. "Short Round, you know I love you like a sister, but you go blabbing to my wife, and I'll sic Alex on you." Alex Lamont just shook his head at his brother's empty threat before turning his attention to Abby.

"Abigail. Sweetness, you seem to have made some mighty important people nervous. What can you tell us that might help us keep you safe?"

Logan appreciated the way Alex had framed his question even if he was surprised at how much the former SEAL had mellowed since becoming a husband and father. Abby stepped up and sat in the space he and Kalen made between them.

"First of all, I want to thank each and every one of you for whatever part you played in my rescue." Logan saw her eyes fill with unshed tears and was proud of her for taking a couple of deep breaths to push the emotion back and get back to the subject at hand. "And you are right, it seems I might have underestimated the threats I'd been getting."

Logan felt his entire body tense and watched as every face surrounding him clouded with the same frown.

"Abby, you better explain yourself quickly before Kalen pops a vein." Zach was smiling at Abby, and she seemed to relax a bit at his words. Logan was sure she'd known the reaction her words were going to get, so he knew it hadn't been easy for her to admit her error.

"Well, it built so slowly, I really thought it was just more of the same political b.s. I have been dealing with since word of my research was first leaked. After the first security breach, I reevaluated my team and made some big changes. I took everyone off my file access list on the server and also pared down my team to the bare bones. It slowed down our progress, but I was sure it was the right thing to do, and both of my dads agreed. There hadn't been any specific threats recently, but the climate on my team changed after two people in my inner circle had bad car accidents. Suddenly, it was as if I had the plague. Now in hindsight, I can see that those left on my team were probably getting pressured to hand over our results. The problem would have been they didn't really have anything other than what they could remember about their small sliver of the information pie, and that wouldn't have been enough for the people pushing for answers. Long story short, I probably set myself up for what happened by making myself the only person who could access the files."

When no one commented immediately on what Abby had said, Logan watched as she seemed to deflate right before his eyes, and he felt the emotion pouring off of her despite the fact he knew she had to be completely spent. Regret, defeat, sadness, and fear were almost pulsing around her.

Hell, even if she'd been well rested, that emotional

soup was a recipe for hitting rock bottom, but when you added in the level of exhaustion she had to be experiencing, it was probably devastating. Her chin dropped to her chest, and when he saw a teardrop splash onto her fingers, he picked her up and sat her in his lap, so she was facing Kalen.

Logan hated that she'd woken up alone in the big bed they intended to share with her. She was completely drained. It was likely she hadn't been sleeping well for weeks if not several months, considering the information she'd just shared. When Logan looked back at the large monitor they'd been using for the conference call, he was relieved to see Mitch Grayson had joined them.

"Hey, Short Round, can you spare me a few minutes? I just want to see if we can get a bit more information about the day you were abducted." Mitch's voice was casual, and Logan was relieved to see Abby look up and smile.

"Hi, Mitch. Wanna play mind games with me?"

Logan had forgotten about the times the two had faced off about Mitch's gifts. Abby, ever the scientific researcher, had insisted Mitch *prove* the validity of his gifts. She'd badgered him relentlessly, and Mitch had held steadfastly to his claim that you couldn't *prove* the existence of many things, so he wasn't obligated to prove his gifts.

During one visit to the ranch, Mitch had waited until they'd all been loading up to leave before turning to Abby and pulling the rug out from under her world by recounting very detailed information about an encounter she'd had with a professor who was giving her trouble. He'd also told her to stay away from another man she'd shown an interest in and told her his unexplained absences were due to a very extensive drug business she most certainly didn't need to be involved with. And that the man was deliberately aligning himself with her because of her ties to Garrett Oil. Mitch described the man, his car, and several of their coffee encounters. Abby had been completely blown away by the accuracy of the information she knew perfectly well he had no reasonable explanation for possessing.

From that day on, she'd referred to his abilities as "Mind Games," and she'd never questioned him again. But she'd been relentless in her research on the topic, according to Mitch. Jace had simply laughed when Mitch had asked him to intervene, telling him simply, "Welcome to my world, Grayson."

"I do indeed want to poke around a bit and see if maybe I can unearth something you've forgotten. Are you game?" Mitch smiled at Abby, and Logan appreciated Mitch's unspoken question. The man was all about informed consent, and Logan knew he wouldn't delve into Abby's memory without her permission.

"Yes, I want to help in any way I can. Here is what I remember. I worked out hard because I was battling with myself about calling Jace. I knew he, Holly, and Gage had only just arrived home, and well, you know."

Mitch's grin told Logan he did indeed know something she hadn't shared with everyone else in the room. *Interesting.*

"Anyway, as I left the gym, I was distracted and suddenly felt as if something had stung me on the neck. Just as I reached up to touch it, my knees started to fold, and I felt arms wrap around me, and I heard two different voices. Everything was mired in different shades of gray after that, but there is something about a uniform and the word *major* that sticks in my mind, for some reason. I don't really remember anything else until I woke up in the trunk. I knew almost immediately where I was, and I remembered that newer, high-end vehicles have latch releases on the inside. Oddly enough, I was lucid enough to realize we'd just turned off from a smooth surface onto a gravel and rutted one, so I assumed that meant they were taking me to a secluded location. There wasn't anything about that information that seemed like it would bode well for me, so that meant I needed to get out of their car quickly. I got ready, and when they slowed down for what felt like a tight curve, I rolled out of the trunk. I didn't even try to reclose it because I knew they'd hear it slam. Hoping the encroaching darkness and the shade from the trees kept them from noticing the lid was no longer latched until I had time to hide, I immediately took to the cover of the trees. Well, I guess the rest of it is pretty obvious." Mitch didn't say anything for what seemed like long minutes but probably wasn't more than sixty seconds.

"The uniform was khaki and not military but someone working for a paramilitary organization. We'll start with local jails and prisons before working outward, but I think we'll find Major Martell fairly quickly. He has serious power issues and was pissed his lackey used his name. He'll roll on whoever hired him because, at his core, he's a chicken shit." Mitch suddenly seemed to break free from whatever he'd been watching in his mind's eye. He'd once described the experience to Logan as watching a video playing in his head. He grinned at Abby.

"You did great Abby. That is really helpful information. Now, I know you are completely spent, please let Logan take you back to bed so you can rest."

Abby softly muttered her thanks before laying her head on Logan's shoulder and closing her eyes. Logan nodded to Mitch before making his way back to the master suite. By the time he got her settled in the bed, she was fast asleep.

He stayed by her side for several minutes just taking in all the minute details that were the essence of Abby Garrett and thanking her guardian angel for looking out for her until they'd gotten to her.

Chapter 13

A BBY WALKED INTO the SH 216, more commonly referred to as the Hart Building on Senate Hill, to present information to the Energy and Natural Resources Committee, surrounded by a security detail befitting the President himself. She had argued until she had been almost blue in the face that their efforts were overkill, but her efforts had been to no avail. She was surprised to see Daniel Lamont leaning casually against a doorframe in the hallway as they approached the meeting room.

"Hey, sweetie, you didn't think I was going to miss this circus did you?" His teasing words made her smile—God, the man exuded charm from every single pore.

"Please tell me you didn't fly in just for this."

"Nah. Catherine had to get her Callie fix. I swear my wife is trying to figure out a way to adopt Ian's beautiful wife despite all the obvious obstacles." Daniel shook his head and smiled. Abby had heard the women had formed an unusually tight bond that was probably partially due to the fact Callie's own mother and sister had all but sold her out to the family of one of the two young men who had raped her. Callie's story was an amazing one, and Abby hoped to get to know her better while she was staying on the island.

Daniel wrapped her in a warm hug and whispered softly, "I've already made a few calls so you won't have to answer questions about your abduction or why you're surrounded by more people than even *you* realize." He gave her a reassuring squeeze, then added in a voice intended to be heard by everyone around them, "Let's let this brilliant young researcher tell these gentlemen what they want to know, so Ian and I can meet our wives for lunch and hopefully, stop them from buying every pink thing in D.C. I honestly believe the two of them believe they decided the baby is going would be a girl, and the Universe aligned itself to comply." His chuckle made Abby smile. Daniel Lamont was obviously still completely smitten with his gorgeous wife even after several decades of marriage.

Abby was pleased her presentation had gone flawlessly, and the committee members' questions had been directed solely at the project and its worldwide implications. But there had been an underlying current of tension flowing through the room that had unnerved her. She finally figured out most of the animosity seemed to be coming from one of the Senators' young aids. The young man was constantly making notations and seemed to be texting or emailing frequently.

Kalen had slid a note to her that simply read, *We're on it*, so she knew they'd noticed his odd behavior as well. Abby had been feeling upbeat about the reception her findings had gotten even though she'd greatly generalized them because technically, all her research and the results were the intellectual property of Garrett Oil. When she had turned to leave the room, she spotted Sergio Fantella at the back of the room and froze in her tracks.

She was immediately surrounded by four very large men, and just as she was ready to tell them she preferred to just leave as quickly as possible, she heard Sergio's accented voice.

"Gentlemen, I assure you I mean Abby no harm. I heard she was going to be speaking today, and I came simply to see for myself that she is alright."

"Who are you, and how do you know Abigail?" Kalen's voice was razor sharp.

"My name is Sergio Fantella, and I work for the Energy Consortium. Abby and I were once friends until I foolishly betrayed her trust by not revealing who I worked for." Abby gently pushed Kalen aside and stepped up in front of Sergio.

"As you can see I am fine. Now, if you'll excuse us, we have lunch reservations." As she attempted to walk past him, Sergio reached out and placed his hand on her arm to halt her. She heard several of the men growl behind her. *Possessive much? Who do they think has been looking out for me all these past several years?* Granted she hadn't been kidnapped then, but still... To his credit, Sergio let go of her immediately and raised his hands in a clear signal of surrender.

"Abby, I want you to know I had nothing to do with your abduction. Yes, I was asked to recruit you, they would still like very much to hire you, but I would never harm you. Never, Brisa, I swear it to you." Abby felt her cheeks flame at his use of the pet name he'd called her because he had insisted she was a breath of fresh air. She was deeply embarrassed by the fact he'd fooled her. She'd really believed he had been interested in her as a woman. She had been totally humiliated to find out she was lusting after him and dreaming about what he'd be like in bed before he confessed he was gay. Thankfully, most of the communication had been electronic, so at least she hadn't made a complete fool of herself face to face.

As she listened to him now, she found herself inclined to believe him. For some reason, his words didn't seem to be untrue, but then she obviously wasn't that good at drawing conclusions related to this man, so she simply nodded, then made her way out of the room.

Grateful none of the men flanking her had tried to stop her or ask her any of the questions she knew were coming, she made her excuses and ducked into the ladies' lounge. She needed a moment to get her bearings and just take a deep breath that wasn't swimming in testosterone. After using the restroom and washing her hands, she realized there was someone standing to her side.

Looking into the mirror, she met the eyes of Tamry Davis, one of the research team she'd cut loose several months ago. Instinctively knowing this meeting wasn't a coincidence, Abby activated the audio on her new bracelet as she dried her hands.

"What are you doing here, Tamry?" Abby knew she needed to stall, and she was more than a little curious about Tamry's role in the drama she felt she'd been cast in. *Damn, I never had any desire to be an actress, and here I am smack dab in the middle of some stinking soap opera.*

"Personally? I don't want a fucking thing from you. Anybody as stupid as you are could never be a friend of mine. You're holding the goose that lays golden eggs in your hands, and you don't even know it. Or worse yet, you know and don't care. Hell, you were born with a silver spoon in your mouth, so you probably really don't need the money."

Abby noted the woman's escalating agitation and wondered just how much higher her voice would go before it started to crackle like static.

Abby refused to take the bait, instead she chose to just wait her out.

"There are bigger players than Garrett Oil, and they'll be in touch soon. I was just sent to make sure you think carefully about how much your precious family means to you. There are several of them who are quite vulnerable, including your new sister-in-law... oh, and she's pregnant too, right?"

Abby couldn't help the snarled face she knew she was making or the string of curse words she uttered that would have made a sailor proud.

"Touch any member of my family, and I'll find you. There won't be a corner anywhere in the world dark enough for you to hide." Abby heard pounding on the door and briefly wondered why the men weren't just bursting through, but obviously, Tamry had locked it from the inside.

The bitch smiled at her after glancing at the door and simply said, "We will be in touch." She turned and walked out a second exit Abby hadn't even noticed. Before Abby could take a step toward the locked door, it shattered, raining splintered wood around the room, and she was quickly surrounded.

Looking up into the furious face of her brother, she merely pointed to the steel panel door that was almost impossible to see unless you knew it was there. At his raised eyebrow, she just nodded, and he immediately started barking orders into a headset he hadn't been wearing earlier and disappeared into the hall. Abby slumped against Kalen, resting her cheek against his chest and tried to calm her wildly beating heart. She felt his arms tighten around her and the kiss he pressed to the top of her head.

"Love, I'm going to be white-headed by the end of the week if this continues." She knew he was only half kidding her, and his attempt at humor had likely taken a Herculean effort. Kalen was intensely protective of all women and had always seemed particularly so with her. Abby could almost feel the tension vibrating around him and knew he was battling to maintain his usual calm in the face of what had been an obvious threat to every member of her family. Suddenly, the reality of what Tamry said hit her, and she started to shake from her very core.

"Where is Holly? Is she alright? Oh God, what about my parents?"

"They are fine, love—all of them. As soon as she made the threat, the guys in the control center on the island started making calls. We've had verbal confirmation from everyone. Now, let's get you out of here. Some of the team is staying behind to try to find that bitch, but we need to get you back to the island."

"Can we stop by my hotel room and pick up my things? I need some clothes." Abby knew by the way Kalen's entire body seemed to bristle, she wasn't going to like what he had to say.

"Your room had been completely cleaned out that first night, love. We sent a team there as soon as we knew where you had been staying, and the room was completely empty. We'll have clothing sent to you. Were there any medications or incidentals you need replaced?"

"No." She hated that her answer sounded so cryptic, but the simple fact was she was beyond pissed. Whoever was behind this bullshit had finally gotten on her last nerve. Stealing clothes? Really? Wasn't that just about as low as a criminal could sink? Thinking about them touching her panties made her want to vomit. She pushed out of his arms and stalked from the washroom and down the hall, ignoring several people who called after her. When Kalen finally grabbed her arm and spun her to face him, she could see the concern and the frustration in his expression.

"I'm sorry, but I'm just plain pissed off. I'm tired of being a damned victim, and I'm completely fed up with these asshats messing up my schedule. They are costing Garrett Oil an ungodly amount of money, and I shudder to think what it's costing Ian. I'm tired and hungry, and I don't have any damned panties." She ended her tirade with a stomp of her foot and looked up in time to see Jace standing a few feet from her smiling.

"Welcome back, Short Round. I've been wondering when you were going to show up. And just for the record—I doubt your men are going to care about the panties." Jace leaned forward and kissed her on the forehead before turning and leading them out the door. A part of Abby was still steaming and more than a little embarrassed by the panties comment. But another part of her wanted to fist pump the air because her brother's "normalcy" had validated her anger and empowered her all in three short sentences. *Still my Indy.*

Chapter 14

JOHN PARSONS LEANED back in his chair and watched the video feed of Abigail Garrett's presentation and wondered how he'd managed to surround himself with so many fools. The woman had slipped through his fingers yet again, and now, she was going to be very difficult to bring on board because her family and friends had dropped an impenetrable net over her. Hell, his CIA details could take lessons from those people.

Sighing, he watched as the tiny hellion finally showed some of the spirit he'd known was lurking beneath her ever-present professional demeanor. *Well, well, finally. Maybe she will break free of the gilded cage all on her own.*

He should have hired someone with less integrity than Fantella to meet the Consortium's "hire her at all costs" dictate. Of course, he'd known they were only talking about offers of money, but the man had chosen to take a broader view of their directive. The bonus the group offered for bringing the young researcher on board had been enough to convince John using a man who already worked for the group was the safest option. Unfortunately, Fantella's sense of honor had proven to be the downfall of what should have been a sure thing.

The two men who flanked the lovely Ms. Garrett as she left the building were obviously interested in her, and her body language indicated she was already at ease with both of them. John knew both Logan Douglas and Kalen Black had been members of the Special Forces and now worked for Ian McGregor because it was his job to know such things. What he hadn't known was the men evidently shared their women because there hadn't been the slightest nuance of jealousy between them.

It seemed that perhaps it was time to take General Franklin up on his offer to introduce him to Alex and Zach Lamont. Finagling an invitation, then walking through the front door of Ian McGregor's exclusive club wouldn't be a challenge, but it wouldn't open the doors he needed opened either. Leaning forward to pick up his phone, he hit the freeze frame on the video feed, capturing Abigail Garrett's look of defiance as she looked around her before settling in the back of the black SUV that whisked away.

Studying her image as he waited for the General's aid to put him through, he was intrigued. She was a study in contrasts, unquestionably brilliant in her research, but naïve in social situations. Gorgeous, but she seemed to be oblivious to her effect on the opposite sex. And there was an undeniable vulnerability hiding beneath her strength. Hell, it was no wonder Sergio Fantella had been so taken with her. Thinking back on all he knew about the Consortium's front man, he didn't remember the man ever being seen in the company of a woman which seemed odd, now that he considered it. He was grateful Franklin finally came on the line before he could easily become lost in his thoughts of Abby Garrett.

ABBY PACED THE living room like the caged animal she considered herself to be at the moment and fumed. Since when did she let a couple of men dictate her every move? Cripes, she was tired of not having anything of her own to wear. Callie McGregor had been more than generous and had literally opened her closet doors, insisting they have their own mini shopping spree because as she'd laughed while pointing at her rounded belly, she wasn't going to be able to wear any of the beautiful clothes Ian had bought for her for quite a while, anyway. Abby loved Ian like a brother, but she damned well wasn't ever going to let him buy her clothes. Crap on a cracker, the man had a serious hard-on for sexy clothing.

Even though she and Callie were close to the same size, their curves weren't in all the same places and what looked seductive on Callie made Abby look like a high-end hooker. And stilettos? Well, you could give that up. Give Abby a comfortable pair of Keen sandals for summer and Ariat boots with her Levis in the winter, and she was good to go. Many of the pieces of clothing Callie had sent her out the door with probably cost more than Abby's entire wardrobe. When she'd complained, Callie had giggled and told her she was singing to the choir because before she'd married Ian, she'd shopped at second hand and thrift stores... when she could scrape together more than a couple of bucks.

They'd made plans to share an early dinner after Ian insisted Callie rest for a while. Abby had giggled when Callie had rolled her eyes behind Ian's back. He'd never turned around, just informed her she'd just earned another punishment, and she could feel free to keep it up because he had plenty of paper. Abby laughed out loud because Katarina Lamont had told her Alex and Zach had made that same promise to her during her first pregnancy and made good on each one of their marks on the tally after the triplets had been born. Kat has sworn she'd just gotten caught back up when she got pregnant again.

Abby couldn't believe Logan and Kalen thought it was reasonable she shouldn't be allowed to leave the island. They surely hadn't been serious about that. Abby had done the calculations, and considering the area of the small piece of real estate that wasn't currently occupied by any type of structure, she figured she would have explored every square inch by the weekend if her pacing had been linear movement. Sure, just before she'd gotten in the SUV outside the Hart Building, she'd had the oddest sense she was being watched, but given today's technology and the fact she was in the nation's capital, it certainly was a reasonable assumption. Something about that moment had made the hair on the back of her neck stand straight up, but she hadn't been able to explain it.

Probably just more evidence of her rapid slide down a slippery slope into insanity. *And do you think anybody gives a rat's ass? Hell, no they don't. All they care about is hiding away the crazy daughter/sister/fuck buddy.* When she finally looked up, she realized both Kalen and Logan were leaning against the wide door leading to the living room, watching her intently. She froze in mid-stride and knew by the sly smiles she must have been rambling aloud. Well, as her new friend Callie would say, *frackin' fairy farts.*

"Fuck buddy? It seems our little sub needs some direction for all of that energy and to be reminded about our dim view of self-depreciating remarks." Logan's leisurely drawl didn't fool her for a minute. She'd known him since she'd been just a kid and knew he could engage that southern charm—complete with accent—at will and always when it served his purpose.

"I'm not taking that sweet southern boy bait, Logan. I know you too well. Jace told me all about how you use that with women." *Uh oh, might have just yanked the tiger's tail there, Abby.* Logan's entire body seemed to go on instant alert, and he didn't look happy… oh no, not happy at all.

"Oh, Abigail, you have gotten yourself into a pretty pickle indeed. You've just accused Logan of treating you like some woman off the street. Hell, I could probably sell tickets to the next half hour's events." Kalen's words might have alluded to humor, but his eyes were telling an entirely different tale. He wasn't happy with her remarks either.

Never one to know the best time to back away, Abby figured *in for a penny, in for a pound.* "Well, whether or not you are thrilled with what my brother told me isn't the question. I noticed you didn't deny it the accuracy of Jace's information." *What? Hell, Abby, you aren't even trying to save your ass.* When her eyes darted to the door, they both chuckled, but it was Logan who started for her.

"Thinking about bolting, baby? Good luck with that. I'm fairly certain two former SEALs can keep one tiny woman contained if they put their minds to it." Abby hadn't even realized she was backing away from Logan until she backed right into Kalen's rock-hard chest and felt his arms tighten around her like steel bands. "See there? Contained. Now, what shall we do about that smart mouth of yours?" Kalen turned her and lifted her over his shoulder before she could blink. They both took off down the hall, completely ignoring her giggling shrieks of protest.

Chapter 15

LOGAN DIDN'T GIVE a tinker's damn that Abby had called bullshit on his accent because she'd been absolutely right. But he had been thrilled she'd handed them the perfect way to distract her on a silver platter. On their way back to the apartment, he and Kalen had talked about ways they could amp things up with her, but they couldn't have planned anything as perfect as what they'd walked into.

"Best stop your squealing before the neighbors come over and watch your punishment, baby. Our neighbors are seriously kinky, ya know."

Kalen set her on her feet and kept a hand on her as she swayed while the blood rushed from her head, but to her credit, she didn't miss a beat.

"Did you just call my brother *seriously kinky*? Because I have to tell you, that's just wrong on so many levels. And my new sister is not kinky, she is merely open-minded. It's just wrong for you to talk about the mother of my niece or nephew in such disrespectful terms... wrong, I tell you. Hey! Are you two degenerates listing to me?" Logan went completely still and saw Kalen had done the same. Turning slowly toward her, he simply raised his brow.

"I'm going to give you one chance to rephrase that statement, Abby, so you might want to think very carefully. Because the next words you say are going to determine whether you get *punishment* or a very real punishment. Keep in mind, there is a significant difference between teasing and blatant disrespect." He saw her eyes go wide and a flash of rebellion before the rational part of her brain decided to overpower the emotional and mouthy part.

"I'm sorry, but you weren't answering me, and I well, sometimes I slip back into our old way of talking to each other, and I forget it's probably not okay since we aren't really friends like that anymore."

He watched her take a deep breath, and the look of defeat in her expression saddened him. *And what did she mean by we weren't friends like that anymore?*

"Anyway, I'm sorry."

Kalen stepped forward and tilted her chin up, so her gaze was focused on them, not the floor. "Love, we value every aspect of our relationship with you, but in the bedroom or anytime we are in a sexual situation we'll refer to as a scene, we'll expect a higher level of respect from you. We'll also expect your complete honesty when answering questions. You'll be expected to answer immediately and without editing or omissions. Communication is the key to any relationship's success and particularly so in one centered around Dominance and submission so any lapses will be dealt with immediately and harshly." When Kalen stepped back beside him, Logan looked at Abby and crossed his arms over his chest.

"Strip." Her gasp of surprise almost made him smile because her internal battle played out so clearly over her expressive face. Desire finally won—she pulled the clingy knit dress over her head and dropped it to the side. Standing there in her lacy white bra that did nothing to hide her peaked nipples and barely-there panties already wet with her arousal, she paused for a few beats. He and Kalen had both helped train enough submissives, they knew she was waiting to see if they had really meant for her to take off everything or not. When neither one of them moved, he saw her swallow, then slowly remove the undergarments.

"Very pretty, baby. Next time, no pausing, understand?"

"Yes."

"When we are in a scene, you'll address us as Sir or Master, and your answers will be complete. Try again." Kalen kept his voice level and his tone neutral—pure "training-mode." He was more of a stickler for protocol as Abby was about to discover.

"Yes, Sir, I understand." Logan hadn't detected any sarcasm in her response, so he decided to move on.

"Bend over the edge of the bed and spread your legs." When she did, he adjusted her position, so her ass was peaked and in the perfect position for his hand. Her pussy lips were exposed, so he could check her arousal and land a couple lighter slaps directly on her sensitive tissues and send her right into orbit when the time was right. Tracing his fingers up and down her spine, he reminded her, "You have two safe words, baby. Tell me what they are and when they are used."

"Yellow means I'm getting close to my limits, and I need things to slow down or to ask a question, and red means I'm past my limits either emotionally or physically, and everything stops." Her voice had already become airy, and Logan could smell her arousal. He ran his fingers through her slick folds, pleased to find she was already soaking wet.

"Very good. Are you ready?" Before she could even answer, he landed four sharp slaps to her ass. The blows weren't as hard as they could have been, for sure, but they would have been much more than she had probably been expecting. He slid his fingers through her pussy again, and she was even wetter than before.

"You did very well, baby. Your pink pussy is even wetter than it was before we started, and that pleases both of your Masters very much." He landed several more blows on each ass cheek, taking care he didn't land the blows in the same place twice. It was obvious she was getting very close to her release, so he backed away to pick up the small butt plug he'd placed on a side table. "This is going to feel cold for just a second, baby." When he dribbled the lube over her rear hole, she only whimpered in need.

While he rimmed her tight rosette with his finger, Kalen moved to the bed, seating himself in front of her, so her face was, for all intents, in his lap. As Logan pushed his finger past the tight outer ring, he leaned over her back, slid his other hand under her, and pinched first one nipple, then the other.

"Suck him, baby. I want to watch his cock disappear between your lips." While she was distracted by Kalen's cock sliding in and out of her sweet mouth and his instructions about what he liked, Logan was able to get two fingers inside her ass, so he quickly moved the plug into place.

"Bear down, baby." When she tensed, he gave her ass two sharp blows, knowing these were the first that would have actually been painful. "No, Abby. There will be times during play your safety depends on following our directions to the letter. It will become more and more important as we explore your limits, so best you get yourself in that mindset now." When she relaxed and pushed back, he quickly seated the plug.

"Very good, baby. Now, we're going to challenge you a bit. I'm going to continue to work over this sweet ass with a flogger while you suck on your other Master's cock. You don't come until you are given permission, and my blows will continue to get harder until you've made your Master come." He leaned down and bit each of her ass cheeks, just enough to draw soft gasps. He loved seeing the light marks he was leaving on her delicate skin. They wouldn't stay long, but for the duration of this scene, she'd be marked as *his*.

The flogger he'd chosen was soft and would feel like soft tickles that turned warm—at least, they would in the beginning. With the first few strikes, she seemed to be far too contented, so he gave her several with a flicked wrist so she'd feel the sting right away. Kalen's head fell back, and his eyes closed when she began to pay closer attention to the details that were going to get her Master off as quickly as possible.

"Fuck, love. You have a devil-blessed mouth. Feeling your tongue caress the tender spot just under the rim is going to send me straight to heaven." Kalen's rough voice was a sure sign Abby was already pushing his control.

Logan slowed the blows, he'd been so caught up in watching Abby making love to Kalen with her mouth. There really wasn't another way to describe the intensity and focus she was bringing to the task.

"It seems our beautiful woman loves giving head, doesn't it, Master Kalen? I can see she is clearly very focused on her 'assignment.' Let's see how multi-tasked she is." Logan tapped the end of the butt plug which turned on the small vibrator to the lowest setting. He smiled when she moaned around Kalen's girth which in turn caused Kalen to groan. Giving Abby several more strikes with the flogger up the backs of both of her thighs, he watched as she began lifting into the blows and knew she had to be getting close to orgasm.

When Kalen gave him the signal he was close to coming, Logan positioned himself at the entrance of her pussy and started teasing her with torturously slow thrusts that barely gained any depth. He heard Kalen telling her to drink every drop and began thrusting in hard and fast. As Kalen shouted his release, Logan pinched her nipples and growled, "Come for us, Abby." When her pussy locked down on him like a velvet vise, she took him right over the edge with her. "Jesus Christ, baby."

Logan hadn't lost control of a release since—hell, he couldn't ever remember being so blindsided by an orgasm. It felt like his balls were being sucked dry, and the aftershocks that electrified every cell of his body almost dropped him despite his locked knees. He swayed on his feet, remembering how intense his connection to Abby felt during the height of the orgasmic wave they'd surfed for what seemed like several minutes. But there was no way he could have accurately judged time—his mind had completely blanked out.

When he finally felt like his brain was getting enough oxygen he would be able to form coherent sentences, Logan pulled his hands out from under Abby and kissed a line across both shoulders before pulling out of her. Her pussy was still rippling with aftershocks, and she moaned in protest at the loss.

"Shhh, baby. I'll be right back. Don't move."

"Can't move. Proly won't ever be able to move again." Her words were slurred and heavy with the husky sound of a well-sated woman, and that warmed his heart. Seeing her red ass and thighs bent over the edge of the bed with the plug still seated above the mini-waterfall of the combined juices from their release now coating her pussy lips and inner thighs burned into the deepest parts of his soul, and he wanted to beat his chest at the sight. Shaking off his wandering thoughts, he quickly cleaned himself and returned to clean Abby before lifting her onto the bed.

Logan couldn't remember ever seeing Kalen so wiped out after a scene. His friend must have noticed his assessment because he shook his head and spoke softly over the beauty sleeping between them.

"She completely decimated me. It's never been like that with any other woman. Honestly, I don't even have words to describe the feelings I have for her. Love is just so inadequate, it's almost an insult to use it."

Logan didn't answer because he'd reached a level of sexual fulfillment with Abby he hadn't even realized was possible, let alone experienced. The one thing he knew above all else was that he couldn't live without her. She was breathing life back into a part of his soul that had died bit by bit over the last several years he'd been a SEAL.

Being sent into every hellhole Uncle Sam could find took a toll on all soldiers, but those on special teams were particularly vulnerable. Special Forces teams worked hard to make sure their members were given plenty of opportunities to work through any mental health issues they had because quite frankly, they were considered very expensively trained assets.

Unfortunately, the simple truth was Special Forces operatives rarely utilized the services of professionals. They feared being removed from their team until some shrink who had never seen a day of battle decided they were "fit" to return. SEALs were taught from their first day at BUDS training to "suck it up and persevere," and that mentality bled over into every aspect of their service. Logan felt like he traded a small part of his soul to the devil every time he was sent on a mission, and he hadn't held out any hope he would ever be able to restore what he'd lost—until he and Kalen made love to Abby.

It wouldn't matter what they had to do to make it work, Logan knew Kalen would agree, nothing was more important than the angel sleeping between them. She was sleeping—truly lost in a deep, restful slumber, something Logan feared she hadn't been doing for a very long time. She was blissfully unaware she'd just tilted their entire world on its axis. Having Abby safe between them and knowing she loved them brought a deep sense of contentment that felt like a warm summer rain as it washed away all the sludge that had been locked in the dark corners of his heart. Logan smiled as sleep pulled him under with promises of sweet dreams for the first time in too long, and it was all because of the tiny woman snuggling like a kitten seeking warmth and comfort between him and Kalen.

Chapter 16

One week later

CALLIE MCGREGOR TAPPED quietly on the doorframe of her husband's office when she heard unfamiliar voices coming from inside. She had walked up from the dock below their house and had noticed a boat she didn't recognize, so she wasn't surprised Ian was in a meeting. What did surprise her was that she'd gotten a text as she'd come in the door, instructing her to come directly to his office.

Checking her appearance in the reflection of the kitchen windows and kicking off her shoes, she didn't even bother setting down the samples she was carrying. She smiled at the feeling of the cool tiles against the bottoms of her feet. Ian wanted her barefoot as much as possible, and certainly, anytime he hadn't specifically asked her to wear shoes when they were at home. She'd teased him about just wanting to be able to say he was keeping her barefoot and pregnant, but he'd growled something along the lines of it being insurance she couldn't run away from him, or at least, that she wouldn't be able to run fast.

When he beckoned her inside, she kept her focus on her handsome Master as she made her way across the room. She might not have been in the D/s lifestyle for a long time, but she understood the importance of not making eye contact with anyone other than Ian until he'd given her permission to do so. The fact he sometimes did, and other times did not was largely dependent upon the visitor, not Callie. He'd explained that he often dealt with people he didn't particularly like, and therefore, he wanted to keep her exposure to them at a minimum. She suspected her loving Master would be even more protective of their child, and that was fine by her.

"*Carlin*, come here." She knew the minute he noticed the packages she was carrying. Jumping to his feet, he took them from her and set them aside. "Tell me why my sweet pregnant sub is carrying her own packages when she knows perfectly well we have staff who would be more than happy to help." His eyes were twinkling, and she knew he'd just given her a hint about the man sitting in one of the leather chairs facing his desk.

Callie suppressed her smile because Ian, without fail, sat single visitors in the chair on his left. The chair on the right was the one he'd sat her in the night he and Jace had caught her sneaking onto the island, and it held special memories for them both. Ian had told her he'd known the exact moment when she had realized the evidence of her arousal was wetting the leather of the chair beneath her. After Ian had showered her to remove the black smudge she'd painted on her face for her unsuccessful under-their-radar entrance, he'd given her one of his shirts to wear. She remembered exactly how cold that leather had felt against her bare pussy and ass, and the fact he didn't like anyone else sitting in *her* chair always made her feel like a warm chocolate sundae inside.

When she blinked up at him, he was smiling down at her, and she was glad she had her back to the other man. She knew from Ian's sly smile, she had spoken at least some of her musings out loud and felt herself flush. He leaned forward, brushing a kiss over her forehead, letting her know he wasn't angry. Turning her around, he spoke over her shoulder, "Callie, this is John Parsons." Before he'd even finished introducing her to the man sitting in front of her, Callie had taken an involuntary step back.

There was something about John Parsons that set off every alarm Callie possessed, and while she didn't know anything about him, she did know he wasn't what he pretended to be—deceit was practically oozing from the man. Ian wrapped his arms around her, and she felt herself shudder.

"I'm sorry, my love, it appears you are more tired than I knew." Turning his attention to the man sitting in front of them, he added, "Excuse me, Mr. Parsons, I'd like to get my lovely wife and child settled. I'll be right back." Ian quickly led her down the hall, then turned her in his arms after closing the door on the master suite.

"Carlin, I'm sorry, but thank you for confirming what Mitch and Logan both said about the man in my office. He was recently introduced to Alex and Zach by a very reluctant General Franklin, and during his first conversation with them, he asked for an introduction and guest pass to Club Isola. Everything about it reeks, but no one knows exactly what he's up to. I know he is *very* highly placed in the CIA, and that's more than I cared to know. Your immediate reaction to him was all the confirmation I needed that something is very wrong here."

Callie hadn't had a chance to get a word in, but she took it in stride, knowing it was a common occurrence with her wonderful husband. His brilliance sometimes came out in a tumbling burst of information. There were times that she knew he might appear to be talking *to her*, but he was actually simply processing information out loud. She also knew he'd have a sudden realization of what he was doing and rectify it quickly by asking her dozens of questions.

She loved him more each day, and she didn't let a single one go by she didn't thank God for the blessing that was now settling her on their bed and covering her with a cashmere throw. He was looking down at her with such love, she couldn't resist taking his hand in hers and pulling it to her lips. Pressing a kiss in his palm, she whispered, "I love you" against his warm skin.

"I love you more. Rest a bit. We're having guests for dinner before we go to the club. I have a surprise for you." His smile was wicked, and she felt her pussy respond with a sudden flood of moisture, and the walls of her vagina contracted. Ian tapped the end of her nose and smiled. Damn, he always knew exactly how he affected her.

"Hold that thought, my love." He pressed his lips against hers, and the kiss she'd expected to be short and sweet turned into a possessive promise of things to come that left her panting for oxygen and desperate for more as he left the room.

ABBY STOOD IN front of the bathroom mirror and studied the outfit Kalen and Logan had given her to wear. The dress—if you could really call it a dress—barely covered her ass, and without panties, it had the potential to be downright obscene. If she hadn't spent an hour over the spanking bench yesterday for asking if they were "fucking serious" about another pseudo-dress they'd brought her to wear, she might have questioned this outfit. Abby liked to think of herself as a quick study—as do most Mensa members—so she decided to can the commentary.

You'll just have to remember not to bend over or take any deep breaths or move. Crapping crickets, this is going to suck.

"What exactly are you planning to suck, baby?" Logan's voice was full of amusement, and his eyes practically danced when she whirled around to find him leaning in the door. Slapping her hand over her heart to try to keep it from jumping right out of her chest, she gasped.

"Holy shit, you scared me half to death. It's not nice to sneak up on people you know… especially when they are acting crazy and talking to themselves." By the time she'd finished, the dots dancing in front of her eyes were starting to fade. Logan nodded once, letting her know he'd heard her without committing or agreeing with her assessment.

"What was that about sucking? You didn't answer my question, Abby." Uh oh, when Logan used her name rather than calling her baby, he was usually in Dom-mode, so she knew this wasn't a time to let her smart mouth out to play. Hell's bells, she still flinched when she sat down. Damn, that wooden paddle they'd used last night had left her with plenty of reminders about the dangers of being flip with your Dom.

"Well… it's going to suck that I can't bend over or move freely tonight without flashing my ass… ets to everyone. I don't much like showing that view to anyone but you and Kalen. And… well, damn, I really don't want to show my girly bits to my brother… geez, that's just not right." Abby felt her shoulders slump, and she hated being negative, but the dress really was too short.

"Abby, look at me." Logan's voice let her know he meant business, so she raised her face to look at him. She hadn't realized he'd stepped right up in front of her. "Do you trust Kalen and I to keep you safe?"

"Yes, always." She had answered immediately because it was the absolute truth.

"Then you'll have to trust us that you are not going to flash your brother tonight." While his words made her feel a bit better, they seemed... odd somehow.

Deciding to let it go, Abby nodded and just said "Thank you" before turning back to the mirror. She was ready to go but needed the distraction because Logan's heated gaze was moving over her in soft strokes that had her pussy weeping already.

"Bend over and spread your legs. I want to check for bruising and get you ready for tonight." Abby didn't hesitate to do as he asked because she really didn't want to show up at Ian and Callie's with her ass glowing from another punishment. "Very good, baby." She felt his cool fingers moving over the heated flesh of her ass and sucked in a breath and jumped when he pressed into one of the spots that was the most tender.

"WE'LL HAVE TO be careful with you tonight, you are showing some signs of significant deep tissue bruising, and we don't like to see that." Logan didn't say it, but he fucking hated it, always had. He never wanted to leave any mark on a woman, punishment or not, that lasted more than an hour or two after a scene. Seeing the dark purple beginning to show on her ass made his stomach turn. Logan knew Kalen was going to be equally upset when he saw it.

"Shit," Kalen's voice sounded behind him, and Logan knew his friend was as unhappy as he was. Hell, Abby was the most important woman in the world, and they'd hurt her. The realization was like a knife to the gut. "Have you treated those bruises yet?" Logan shook his head and watched as Kalen gathered supplies from the cabinet.

Logan didn't like the idea that the bruises would probably get a lot worse before they got better over the course of the next day or two, and now, what they had her wearing to dinner tonight was a real Catch-22. If they had her change into something long enough, it would cover the marks, and the message to her would be they were trying to hide what they'd done from their friends. And if they let her go in the dress she was wearing, she was going to be uncomfortable, knowing everyone was looking at her, wondering what she'd done, and what the fuck they'd been thinking. Kalen and Logan both began massaging arnica gel into her ass cheeks and the backs of her thighs.

"Love, we are sorry for this. We should have checked you closer this morning, hell, we shouldn't have kept you on the bench so long last night when we really didn't know how your body would react."

"I have always bruised easily. I'm sorry I was so snarky." Logan heard Abby's hisses of pain as she'd spoken and wondered again what they should do about her clothing. "Can I ask a question, please?"

"Yes, baby. What's your question?"

"Could I maybe find something a bit longer to wear, so everybody doesn't figure out what a bad sub I am? It would be kind of embarrassing for you, and since I'll have to be returning to Houston soon, I don't want to leave having everybody thinking I got sent away."

Logan could tell Abby was fighting to hold back her

tears, and he fucking hated hearing the defeat in her voice. *Leave soon? Sent away? Is she kidding? Of course, she isn't kidding, we've kept her locked up in this damned apartment for most of the past week, and she has to be going completely stir-crazy.*

Logan was grateful Kalen had turned her to face him because, at this point, he wasn't sure he had it in him to be rational, and most of his frustration was directed inward.

"Love, I understand about a longer dress, and I think it's a fine idea, but not for the reason you do. No one will think you are a bad sub, but they'll damned well wonder why your Doms had their heads up their asses. I want you to know that us caring for you and wanting you is not predicated on you being a good submissive. Fuck, it isn't even dependent on you *being* a submissive. We want the brilliant and vibrant woman you are inside. And sadly, for this past week, we've done *nothing* to prove that to you."

Kalen's words were exactly right in Logan's view. They'd kept Abby locked up away from the work she loved. Hell, she hadn't had anything but the most minimal contact with anyone but them. She'd talked with her family on the phone and had jogged the paths of the island several times, but that certainly wouldn't be enough to keep someone as smart as Abby challenged. It was a given, she wouldn't be happy unless her mind was working, and she was contributing in some way.

There hadn't been any significant developments in the investigation of her kidnapping, but Logan didn't really expect them to unravel it quickly. Government agencies investigating one another was always a recipe for foot-dragging and competing agendas. Cover-ups were the norm rather than the exception, and Logan doubted this instance was going to be any different.

Logan turned her to face him. "Abby, one of the purposes of tonight's dinner is to discuss Ian's plan to start another club in Houston. He's been planning on expanding for some time but hadn't picked a location. We asked him to consider something in the hills west of Houston and that he transfer us both there so we could be close to you." When he saw her excited expression, he held up his hands.

"Hold on. It's not a done deal yet, it's still being considered, and I don't want you to get your hopes up just yet. The point is, we don't expect you to give up your lab or working at Garrett Oil. From what Ian said, your parents have been thinking about relocating the company headquarters closer to the ranch so your dads wouldn't have such a long commute so it would be perfect."

He wasn't sure exactly what he'd expected her to say, but the longer she just stood there, the more nervous he became. Damn, he wished she'd say something, hell anything would be better than this silence. Logan had been in the SEALs long enough to read body language and anticipate the moves of an opponent, regardless of their age, gender, or culture. But Abby took him completely by surprise when she sprang straight up into his arms—hell, he hadn't even seen her bend her knees. He caught her easily, and when his hands cupped her bare ass cheeks, she hissed which made he and Kalen laugh. She was kissing him like there was going to be no tomorrow and leaned over to do the same to Kalen.

When he finally set her down, he turned her back to the cabinet and nodded to Kalen. He saw Abby's eyes go wide when she saw the items Kalen laid out on the countertop. Logan lifted the dress over her head and bent her at the waist, so her hands were resting on the counter. "Arch your back and push your ass out. We're going to play a bit during dinner, oh, and don't you dare come without permission."

Chapter 17

KALEN ALMOST LAUGHED out loud at the look on Abby's face when she saw the flesh colored butt plug and Ben Wa balls. She was going to be even more surprised when she found out they were both remote controlled and that he and Logan each had one of the controllers in their pocket. They had purposely mixed up the two small remotes, so even they didn't know which device they were controlling.

Once she was in position, Kalen began lubing the plug and rimming her rosette. After spending several hours with this plug stretching her beautiful rear hole, they knew she'd be ready to take them both at the same time when they got home. They were just going to do a quick walkthrough of the club on the way back to the apartment. Logan and Kalen had already arranged for two of their friends to be double fucking one of the club's more experienced subs during their quick tour to set the mood.

They'd seen Abby talking to Lizzy late one afternoon when she'd been out running. The young woman had just been arriving at the club's dock as Abby had been running past, and they'd struck up a conversation that had lasted several minutes. Abby had come bouncing back into the apartment, excited she'd made a new friend and told them all about Lizzy.

They'd both laughed later at her "news" because they had known Lizzy Jantz for a couple of years and had done her background investigation for club membership, so there wasn't much about her they didn't already know. One thing Abby learned that was news to them was Lizzy was being transferred to Texas in a couple of months. She'd told Abby she had recently gotten a promotion and would be taking over a small FBI field office near the western edge of Houston. Lizzy had been happy to be the creamy center for tonight's show after she'd learned it was intended to help Abby see exactly what was going to be expected of her.

Watching the largest of the butt plugs they'd bought for Abby breach her ass was making him so hard, he was worried he might have to find a bit of relief before they left for dinner. He tried to view the encounter as a training session at the club, but it wasn't helping at all thanks to Abby's soft moans and sighs as he kept fucking it deeper and deeper into her ass. Once it was fully set into place, he used his fingers to finger the lips of her labia and smiled at her in the mirror.

"Abigail, you are amazing, and I can hardly wait for tonight's games to begin. But first, Master Logan has another toy for you."

Kalen stepped back and watched as Logan slipped the Ben Wa balls deep into Abby's vagina. Logan leaned down and bit down on the sensitive place where her shoulder joined her neck. They had quickly discovered that spot and the palm-sized spot at the base of her spine were two of their best bets to setting her on fire.

Anytime they were walking next to her, one of them kept his hand on her lower spine, just barely above the crack of her ass. She had freely admitted *that* touch was one of her favorite things, and they were happy to oblige because it also sent a clear signal of possession to every other man watching. Abby might have seen it as comforting or protective, but it had a much more powerful meaning in Kalen's mind—it was the equivalent of his inner three-year-old screaming *Mine*.

When they stood Abby up, she wavered for just a few seconds before he saw her eyes glaze over, and the audible moan that came from her lips sounded like something right out of every porn movie he'd ever seen as a teenager.

"Jesus, baby, give a guy a break, please." She looked up at Logan, her confusion clearly written on her face. "The sounds you are making are mainlining straight to my cock, and I'm going to have to relieve it if you don't stop."

Abby looked between them and then down at the bulges pushing against their leathers. "I could help you with that, you know? Would my Masters enjoy knowing their sub had already had her appetizer when they walked her through their boss's door?"

Kalen stepped up, and in truth, he was grateful for her misbehavior because even though her intention hadn't been to top from the bottom, it was exactly what she'd just done.

"Abigail, that is what Doms call topping from the bottom. It means you are trying to control the situation." He saw her eyes go wide and realization dawn in them. "Oh, love, I know that wasn't your intent, so you'll get a pass this one time. But rest assured, if you do something like that again, there will most certainly be consequences. Now, let's find something else for you to wear, shall we?" *Hopefully, the distraction will be enough to keep me from blowing a gasket before we even get a chance to start.*

In no time, they had Abby dressed in a low-cut dress

that reminded Kalen of orange sherbet. Its soft material flowed around her in soft waves of iridescence. The color was a perfect accent for her golden-brown skin and dark hair, and it was long enough, the bruising that had already become even more evident was covered.

They'd given her shoes to wear but reminded her she would leave them just inside Ian and Callie's front door. Kalen knew Ian *always* kept Callie barefoot inside their home. Hell, he rarely let her wear anything at all when they were in their home alone and before her pregnancy, she'd also been nude even when trusted members of the staff or club were visiting.

When he and Logan stopped at Ian's yesterday after-noon to discuss the possibility of a new club in Texas, Callie had been standing in the corner in Ian's office. Now that she was pregnant, Ian often dressed her in one of his button-down shirts. Yesterday she'd been dressed in a crisp white shirt with blue stripes which was pulled up in the back to display bright red handprints on her bare ass.

Logan raised his brow in question, and Ian had nodded his head in her direction. Kalen watched as his friend walked up beside Callie. "Sugar those are lovely handprints on your beautiful ass, but those tear tracks down your pretty cheeks don't make me think this was fun and games for you. What happened?"

Ian had sighed at her silence, shaking his head. "Carlin, it is alright for you to answer Master Logan's question."

Callie turned to Logan and looked at Kalen as if she'd lost her very last friend. "My Master felt I was too chatty with some of the workers at the Lodge, and I disagreed." So at least that explained her original refusal to answer Logan's question—she was still rebelling, and Ian had known it. Kalen bit back a smile because he was sure she'd be getting a couple more swats for her defiance after they left.

Kalen could see Logan was barely managing to hold back his grin. "Well, sugar, if I was betting I'd say it was the disagreein' part that got you that spanking and not chatting up the workers, am I right?"

Callie had slowly nodded her head, then dropped her gaze to the floor before whispering, "Yes, Sir."

"Sugar, look at me." When she looked up at him again, her eyes were once again filled with tears. "Do you trust your Master to know what is best for you? Do you believe he is always thinking about your safety as well as your happiness?" When she just nodded, Logan had waited, looking at her expectantly until she'd answered him with the words she knew were required. "So why did you disagree with him?"

"Because he seemed so angry, and I was afraid he was going to send me away like... well, like my mom." Callie's words were so soft, Kalen had barely heard her, but Ian certainly hadn't missed them.

Kalen knew this had been a huge hurdle for Callie and one she was obviously still dealing with. Everyone had warned Ian that Callie's self-confidence and security had been so seriously damaged by her mother and sister's betrayal and continuing rejection, her *recovery* was going to be a process. Even though this seemed like a step backward for her, Kalen hoped Ian would remember it was a relatively small step when he considered all the progress she'd made. Before Ian could stalk toward her, Kalen had grabbed his forearm and spoke softly enough, only his boss had been able to hear him.

"It's just a small step back, Ian. Remember the hormone cocktail her body is coping with every minute of every day is powerful stuff. She *needs* you, now more than ever." When Ian seemed to calm, Kalen added, "We'll be back in two hours to talk."

Logan had moved her pretty blonde hair behind her ear and held the side of her face as he spoke soft words of encouragement to her. Kalen watched Logan kiss her on the forehead and turn her into Ian's open arms. The sound of her quiet sobs as they left the room had sent both Kalen and Logan to the gym for a brutal workout. Everybody who met Callie McGregor fell in love with her and seeing their tiny friend in so much emotional pain had shaken the two of them.

"Before Abby, I probably wouldn't have handled that the same way. But now, seeing Callie's pain was hard because I kept thinking about how I'd feel if that was our woman."

Kalen couldn't have agreed more, and he was glad they'd had the chance to help their friends over what could have been a very rough stretch of road.

"It all comes down to communication. I know it's cliché, but it is even more important in D/s relationships because of the power exchange involved. Callie should have told Ian why his criticism was such a problem for her, but Ian should have listened with his heart as well." Kalen didn't have any idea how Ian kept up with Callie when he was sure it was going to take everything *both* he and Logan had to keep up with Abby—and he hoped like hell they were going to be able to stay at least a step or two ahead of her.

Chapter 18

T HERE WEREN'T ANY cars allowed on the small island, so they'd taken one of the electric carts over to Ian and Callie's. As soon as they'd entered, Abby had taken off her shoes, then Callie had spirited her away to show her the *almost* complete baby wing. Her new friend was so excited, Abby was soon caught up in her enthusiasm. They had all teased Ian that most people remodel a room or add on one or two small rooms, but he had added an entire wing for the child Callie was carrying.

When the men finally caught up with them, both she and Callie were sitting in rockers, simply looking at the beautiful view. The moonlight was dancing over the water between the small island and the mainland, and it was what Abby had always thought of as "travel brochure" perfect.

Abby had noticed there was a sense of peace and tranquility that seemed to surround Callie today that had been missing for several days. While Abby didn't know what had changed, she was happy that, for Callie's and her baby's health, her sweet friend seemed to be in a much better place. Callie was getting very close to her due date, so Abby had assumed she was just feeling anxious about all the life changes headed her way.

By the time they all returned to the dining room, Ian's cook and housekeeper was just setting the last of their dinner on the table. Inez patted Callie's baby bump and said, "Miss Callie, you need to feed that baby, so he gets big and strong."

Ian gave Inez a mock stern glare, "Inez, I keep telling you that baby is going to be a girl and just as sweet and beautiful as her mama." Inez merely shook her head at her boss and headed back into the kitchen. Ian had laughed and told them neither he nor Callie actually knew the sex of the baby and hadn't wanted to find out. With only a couple of weeks to go, he laughed, saying he finally realized he was going to survive not having any *control* over whether it was a boy or girl.

Kalen and Logan had just seated Abby between them and shown her how they wanted her ankles hooked around the legs of her chair, so her pussy was open to their touch when she felt the butt plug start to vibrate and gasped. She'd been grateful the others had been busy chattering about the baby and hadn't seemed to notice, but she was certainly finding it hard to track the conversation and was worried she was going to leave a wet spot on the chair when she got up, not to mention what was going to happen to her dress.

Logan leaned over and whispered, "Didn't you notice the towels you and Callie are both sitting on, baby? Lift up your dress and put that sweet bare ass and pussy back down on the towel." When she'd done as he'd asked as discreetly as she could, he'd grabbed one knee, and Kalen had taken the other, as they spread her legs back apart. "Keep you your ankles hooked around the legs of the chair, or we'll bring in one of the taller stools, and you'll be much more *exposed* than you are now."

She felt the cool air drift over her exposed pussy lips again and just as she was starting to feel like she could refocus on what was going on, she noticed Callie seemed to be having similar problems since her head was leaned back against her chair, and she was biting her bottom lip so hard, Abby was worried she was going to draw blood.

"*Carlin*, focus. You are alarming Abby." Ian's sly smile told her he didn't give a rat's ass about her alarm, and she wanted to reach over and "box his ears" as her mother would say. When she glared at Ian, the vibrations of the butt plug kicked up, and Abby felt her entire body stiffen.

"Glaring is rude, Abigail. Keep in mind, Ian is not only our host, he also happens to be a Dom. Not someone you want to cross, and I believe you are already dealing with challenges sitting comfortably."

Abby heard his words, but he might as well have been speaking Pekinese, no make that Portuguese... *fuck it, who cares?* She really didn't care how or what he'd said because her pussy was quickly soaking the towel she was sitting on, and it was getting harder and harder to stave off the tidal wave that was building within her.

Ian's voice broke through the fog clouding Abby's mind. "John Parsons will be visiting the club tomorrow night," was all she'd picked up, but it had been enough. Shaking her head to clear her thoughts, Abby turned to Ian.

"The John Parsons who works for the CIA? Well, I guess he probably doesn't advertise that fact unless he's trying to impress you with his 'position of power.'" She'd used her fingers to put air quotes around her last words and rolled her eyes in obvious disgust at the man. "Why? I mean, why is he coming here? Why now? Has he ever tried to visit the island before I was here? Have you actually met him? Does Jace know this? How did you meet him, anyway?" Ian was watching her with a smile that told her she was amusing him, but both Kalen and Logan had gone on point.

Abby felt herself slip into her "zone" for the first time in weeks, and the familiarity of that place where her mind was totally focused on the task at hand was comforting. Without even realizing she'd done it, she pushed out of her chair and broke the connection between herself and Logan and Kalen. She sent them both apologetic smiles when she realized why she suddenly felt cold.

Stepping away, Abby began pacing back and forth along the windows overlooking Ian and Callie's beautifully landscaped backyard. Her mind had always processed information and brainstormed best when she was moving. She had finally taken the carpet out of her office at the lab because she'd worn it out several times and having it replaced was a major pain in the ass.

Speaking more to herself than anyone else, Abby let herself work through everything that was suddenly tumbling through her mind. Out of the corner of her eye, she saw Kalen start to get up, but Ian put out his hand to still him. She heard Ian say, "Leave her. Let her work it through. It's how her mind operates, and the three of us together can't begin to analyze the data her mind can process." Somewhere in the back of her mind, Abby was pleased with his remarks because Ian McGregor was a genius in his own right. Sure, his genius was "different" from hers, but there wasn't any doubt, it was equally impressive.

Abby slipped back into her own mind and went to work pulling together all the pieces of the puzzle the past six months had been and started arranging them like bits of a jigsaw puzzle in her mind as she tried to see the larger picture.

"It's the voice... more than anything... it's that the

voice of the communication was just so similar. You know how you can recognize an author by the voice they bring to their work? Yes, well, it's the same thing in business and scientific communities. You can tell who wrote an article or letter or e-mail, just by the voice. He's movie star gorgeous, but he's a slime with the most negative aura and energy of anyone I've ever been around. How did he get invited here? And why now? There are no coincidences, Abby. Remember Granny's words... and remember she was *always* right."

IAN WATCHED ABBY pace the length of the large, open space that made up most of the main living area of his home as her brilliant mind processed information at the speed of light. He'd always loved watching the little pint-sized genius work and had stopped her brother from corralling her one night in an elegant restaurant because Ian had known exactly what she was doing. He had installed long strips of cushioned flooring in front of the windows in each of his offices because he was prone to the same method of focusing his thoughts. If he was truly baffled by a problem and working through it in his mind, he had to be moving.

Once Kalen and Logan stepped out of their roles as her Doms and realized what was happening, they had been able to settle back and simply watch the wonder that was Abby Garrett. Ian smiled at their expressions of pride and awe. The sight of her in what Jace had often jokingly referred to as "Full-on Abby" was something to behold. It wasn't until he heard her say something about bait and Mitch Grayson, Ian zeroed in on her words and interrupted her.

"Abby." When she didn't break stride, he tried again but used a voice that was laced with the Dom tone he knew she would instinctively respond to. *"Abby. Stop."* He smiled and shook his head when she halted and turned to him, blinking her eyes as if she were trying to focus on his face. "Sweetness, tell me what you meant about bait and Mitch." He knew she was really back with them when her eyes darted between the two men who had claimed her as their own before returning to him.

"Well, I am fairly sure he is coming here to see me... and *see* might be misleading because, unless I'm totally off the mark, there is a connection between John Parsons and The Consortium... and it's financial. Something Sergio said in one of his last e-mails puzzled me, but now... well, now it makes sense."

Ian knew better than to interrupt her with questions and was grateful that the others in the room took their cues from him. Kalen and Logan might have had more social interaction with Abby Garrett, but he'd actually had more intellectual and professional contact with her, so he appreciated their willingness to let him work this through with her. When he didn't respond, he knew she would continue, and he wasn't disappointed. She explained questions she had regarding e-mail communications and how the "voices" had been too similar to be coincidental.

"Sergio made the comment 'everything changed when I got to know you,' and that had stuck in the back of my mind because it hadn't made sense until I saw him a few days ago. I think he was sent to contact me, but then he got to know me and didn't follow through on whatever he was supposed to do. We actually did have a lot of fun together, and he was obviously interested in my work, but he never pushed me."

Ian watched Abby's muscles twitch and fought his smile—it was obvious she was restless, and standing still while her mind whirled was torture.

"Tell us about John Parsons." Kalen's question had been quietly spoken, almost as if he was afraid of spooking her. Abby smiled at Kalen.

"He is a snake. I know that seems over simplistic, but that's the bottom line. He uses his looks to charm people, but he is pure predator underneath that pretty boy veneer. I wish Mitch could be here because I think his gifts would be very helpful. And yes, in answer to the questions I see in all of your eyes, I intend to be front and center when he visits the club tomorrow night because that is the only way we'll know what he's up to."

Ian heard Callie's small gasp when Abby put her hand up in a universal sign for *stop* when Kalen started to interrupt her.

"Hear me out, Kalen. I'm not a shrinking violet you can keep under wraps and shelter from every storm... even though I love you for wanting to. I've been taking care of myself for a very long time, and I've stood up to Parsons before. Besides, we all know Ian and Mitch are going to cover me in gadgets."

Ian smiled to himself. *Indeed we will sweetness, indeed we will.*

Chapter 19

A S FAR AS Logan was concerned, the entire evening had been FUBAR almost from the beginning. It wasn't that he was totally rigid—hell, he'd had plans that were fucked up beyond all recognition plenty of times. Being able to think on his feet and make adjustments had saved his life too many times to count, but this was definitely different because this time, it was Abby's life hanging in the balance.

They'd planned to play in Ian's playroom to help Abby become accustomed to being seen by someone other than her two Doms, but no one had missed how fast Callie faded after their discussion about John Parsons. As they'd been leaving, she'd been dead on her feet, and Logan felt awful for their part in her exhaustion.

"Sugar, I'm sorry things didn't work out the way we'd planned them. You'd have gotten some much-deserved attention and been in a more comfortable position." He'd waggled his eyebrows at her and was pleased when she giggled. He leaned down and pressed a kiss to her rounded belly and felt the muscles contract beneath his palms. "Sugar are you having Braxton-Hicks contractions?" When she looked at him in curiosity, he smiled. "Hey, I have three older sisters. This isn't my first rodeo."

Logan looked up and saw the look of panic in Ian's expression over Callie's tiny blond head. "It's too early. Oh God, who should we call?" When he pulled out his phone, Logan laughed—loudly.

"Chill out, Ian. They are perfectly normal. Callie's body is just starting to prepare itself for the main event, but she does need to get off her feet and rest more." He leaned down and spoke to the baby, "Be nice to your sweet mama and stop scaring your daddy." Abby pulled Callie into a hug and made her promise to call no matter what... day or night if she needed anything at all.

"Remember, I don't have any sisters, so I need every learning opportunity I can get if I'm ever going to catch up with Logan. I can't have him being smarter than me... that will just *never do*." Looking down, she added, "And you, sweet baby... let your mama rest, but if you really want to make an appearance before I have to leave... so I can hold you...well, I promise not to raise a stink about it." Ian slapped his hand to his forehead in mock horror, then hugged her.

Logan knew Abby hadn't noticed that during her pacing, they'd shut off both toys still seated inside her hot little body. As soon as he'd settled her on his lap for the trip back to the club in the small electric cart, they reminded her by activating both vibes at the same time. Abby gasped and almost slid off his lap, making him grateful he secured the cart's seat belt over them both before they'd taken off. He tightened his arms around her and licked the sensitive spot behind her ear.

"What's the matter, baby?"

"Oh God. Have mercy, please. It's too much. It... it robs me of my ability to think." Her voice was airy, and Logan knew she was scrambling to form coherent thoughts which she wouldn't be able to do for much longer.

"Tell me." Logan's voice was roughened by flaming desire, but he wanted her to learn to verbalize what she was feeling because it would heighten her arousal and also help them to know what was working and not working with their beautiful sub.

Logan had both remotes in his pocket and lowered the settings so she would be able to talk to them. He didn't want her coming as Kalen drove them over the rock path— they wanted to provide that pleasure tonight, not a mechanical device.

"Remember blowing the seeds of a dandelion and letting the wind scatter them when you were a kid? That's what you're doing to my thoughts... just being near you challenges me, but this? Oh, this robs me of my ability to think about anything but how much I want you... both of you... inside me." There wasn't a sound sweeter in the world than hearing Abby's sweet gasps as she tried to focus through the sensations bombarding her unless it was her confession about how much she wanted them. Oh, she'd told them before, but they were never going to get tired of hearing it.

Logan sealed his lips over hers and simply tried to enjoy the taste of her as he slipped his tongue into her sweet mouth. He tried to rein in the rampant escalation of desire he felt when her tongue matched his stroke for stroke, but the power of their connection was simply too strong. The passion pulsing around her was almost enough to make him want to bypass their tour of the club, but he knew it was important to experiment just a bit. This was a perfect chance for them to find out exactly how interested she might be in "broadening her horizons."

Pulling her hands behind her, Logan was able to encircle both of her small wrists with one hand. The position caused her to arch her back upward, pressing her tight nipples against the soft fabric of her dress—the thin material did nothing to hide the pinpoint proof of her arousal.

"Well, Master Kalen, it seems our lovely sub needs a bit of an edge in order to make all the pieces fit together. If you check, I'll bet you are going to find she is soaking wet."

Kalen reached over and moved her dress aside, so he and Logan could both watch his fingers slide through her wet pussy. Kalen slid two fingers in until he encountered the balls they'd left there. "Love, your pussy is drenching my fingers, and that is with those balls in place. You enjoy the restraint, don't you?"

"Oh, yes… please" was all Abby was able to say before Kalen withdrew his fingers. Logan watched her eyes flare with heat when she saw Kalen stick his fingers into his mouth and savor her honey.

KALEN HAD NEARLY driven off the path several times on the short drive from Ian's to the club's back entrance. Watching Abby's response to a small bit of bondage and how much it had seemed to focus her attention on Logan's kiss had been very valuable information indeed. Now, as they walked through the doors of the club, he and Logan would be paying close attention to every reaction from their sweet girl.

"Abigail, I want to remove the Ben Wa balls, so we can finger fuck you if the mood strikes us as we look around a bit." Leading her over to the bar, he winked at Mike Tate who was at his usual post behind the bar. Mike's wife and submissive, Dee was standing at the other end of the bar, trying very hard to not lift her eyes and watch what they were doing with Abby.

"Okay, I'll just go to the ladies room and—"

"No, Abigail. Here. Now. Bend over and grasp the edge of this stool." Kalen interrupted her because she had totally misunderstood what he'd been telling her. When she just stared at him with a stunned expression, he had to bite the insides of his mouth to keep from laughing at her. "Now, love or I'll figure out something you'll like even less."

"Less? Really? There could be something worse? You can't be serious. I can't flash my bare ass to a room of strangers." Little did Abby know she was playing right into their hands. As if on cue, Mike placed a folded towel on the bar and slid it down to him. Kalen knew Abby hadn't missed the movement in her peripheral vision, but she'd kept her focus on him. *Smart girl... mostly.*

Kalen put his hands on her waist and easily lifted her up and sat her on the folded towel, then scooted her, so she was between two bar stools. Logan placed one of her bare feet on one stool and did the same with the other foot. Kalen then slid her forward until her ass was on the very front edge of the bar and simply watched her without speaking for several seconds. Her eyes were wide in surprise but dilated with arousal, her pulse was beating fast at the base of her throat, and her respiration was already fast and shallow. *Perfect.*

"Lean back on your elbows, Abigail, and I'm going to caution you, failure to follow my order is going to earn you a punishment that will be administered immediately, so think carefully, my love." He saw her eyes go impossibly wide before they flashed with heat and a raw desire he'd yet to see from her. For several heartbeats, he held his breath, hoping he hadn't overplayed his hand, but she slowly leaned back. Abby never took her eyes from his as if their gazes had been fused together by the heat of the moment. When he lifted the hem of her dress to her waist, baring her to the room, she squeezed her eyes closed.

"Open your eyes, love. You are in this position because you refused to comply with an earlier order and the challenge you threw down about nothing being worse. I doubt you'll make those same mistakes again even though Master Logan and I are enjoying very much showing you off a bit."

Logan leaned close to her. "Your pussy is beautifully swollen and a luscious shade of dark pink, baby. We love it bare to our touch and view. Every Dom in the room who sees you is going to want what we won't let them touch. Kalen and I only share with each other, sweetheart." Kalen saw her muscles relax just a fraction and knew Logan's words had done exactly what he'd intended. It was common for subs to worry about being passed around the first time their Master bared them to the room, particularly when the scene hadn't been planned in advance, and even though this scene had been planned meticulously, Abby hadn't been privy to any of those details.

Kalen started sliding his fingers through her wet folds, moving from her clit all the way to the edge of the butt plug. After several slow passes, Abby's arousal level was peaking so quickly, he gave her pussy a swat.

"No coming without permission, love." When Kalen glanced to his side, he saw Dee Tate standing nearby as if she'd been frozen in place, her blush clearly visible despite her mocha-colored skin, and Mike's gaze was fixed on her. If Kalen had to guess, he'd put his money on a repeat of this scene with Dee in the near future because the pretty little sub was obviously very turned on by what she was witnessing. Even though his friends had been married for several years, their play had been much less public until recently. Dee's friendship with Callie had helped her come out of her shell, but then Callie seemed to have that effect on everyone.

Sliding his fingers into Abby's channel, he grasped the small string that held the balls together and pulled them out so slowly, he heard Abby's groan over the pounding music playing in the next room. Logan wrapped them in a small handkerchief and stuffed them in his pocket. Kalen licked his fingers clean, then held out his hand to her and was pleased when she placed one small hand in his palm. He pulled her upright, then slammed his lips over hers in a kiss meant to show her exactly how much he wanted her. Breaking apart only when his need for oxygen demanded it, he turned her to Logan and watched his friend use even less finesse.

Subs frequently raved about Logan's ability to seduce with nothing more than a kiss and several had sworn he could make them come from talking or kissing alone, but *this* kiss was about possession and a declaration of ownership to everyone watching. His action practically screamed this woman might not be wearing their collar yet, but she was theirs in every way that counted. Her collar had been delivered today, and they were planning to give it to her later tonight.

Ian's jeweler had created an amazing interwoven pattern of titanium, platinum, and gold, set with diamonds and rubies that also held GPS "gadgetry" as Ian had referred to it. The technology wasn't even on the market yet. The military had first dibs, then it would be made available to the general public.

The locking mechanism was so well hidden, it was virtually undetectable, and he and Logan would have the only keys. The composite of the various metals and patented lock guaranteed no one was removing the collar from Abby without one of the keys. After her primary and secondary trackers were removed by her kidnappers, they weren't taking any chances.

Leading Abby through the club's main room, they reminded her they wanted to hear her thoughts and impressions of the scenes she was seeing. They looked on as a Dom spanked his sub over a spanking bench with a wide paddle. He stopped several times to check with the sobbing woman making her repeat her safe word. She was apologizing for not trusting him to make some decision for her and for being disrespectful. Kalen didn't know the young couple well but knew they were experienced players, so he hadn't worried when he'd seen them on the schedule. Before they'd moved on, the sub was screaming her release when her Master commanded she come for him.

Abby was fascinated by the Shibari demonstration but shuddered when they told her how long it often took to complete. The club's Shibari artist was also a well-known photographer whose portraits were acclaimed as artistic masterpieces and highly sought after. Kalen had never considered buying one because the thought of spending hundreds of thousands of dollars for a picture of someone else's woman held no appeal for him. He noticed the rattan backdrops and knew Keagan would be taking photos tonight and smiled because the young woman modeling for him was about to make a whole lot of money. When the first flash went off, Abby's eyes widened in disbelief.

"I wouldn't have thought Ian would let anyone in with a camera. Aren't there privacy concerns?"

"No, love. Keagan Sato is an internationally known artist. Ian will screen every shot before he leaves the island. They are longtime friends, and Ian trusts Keagan implicitly. If you are worried about the model—don't. She will be well cared for, and Keagan pays them lavishly for their time and gives them a nice share of the profits from their pictures. The young woman he is working with tonight has funded her entire college education working with Keagan. You can't really see her well, but she is stunning. Her father was a light-skinned African American soldier and her mother a Japanese model. Sunni inherited the best traits of both cultures and recently completed her residency in neurology."

Kalen barely managed to hold back his chuckle when he heard Abby's softly uttered words.

"Must be why she can use mind over matter to keep from having to pee. I'd never make it."

Chapter 20

KEEPING HIS HAND against the small of Abby's back, they approached the last scene they'd planned to show her, and Logan felt her go rigid at the sight. At first, he was worried she was going to turn and run, but it quickly became clear arousal rather than fear caused her reaction. Their friends were in one of the more private observation rooms. The curtained wall had been opened, so the threesome was visible from the viewing area but there was only one other ménage group watching, and from the looks of things, they wouldn't be there much longer.

Logan had been pleased when he'd learned Tony Dent and Don Whiteside had become friends. Tony had been a Navy SEAL, but after he'd lost the bottom portion of his leg after a shrapnel injury, he'd opted to resign his commission rather than take the desk job he knew he'd be assigned. Don Whiteside was the surgeon who had treated Holly, and even though she still referred to him as Dr. Donnie Dark, Jace swore she was warming up to him—finally. Both Doms were tall and had dark complexions due to their Italian heritage, but that was as far as their similarities went as far as Logan could tell.

Dr. Whiteside's name was a complete irony, and Logan tended to think Holly's nickname for the man might well be more appropriate. His kinks were skating close to sadism, and he'd put every dungeon monitor and member of the security team on the edge of their seat more than once. Several of them had taken their concerns to Ian in the beginning, but their boss had assured them he knew exactly who he was dealing with and granting him a lifetime membership to Club Isola had not been a mistake. As it was turning out, the man seemed to have a wide latitude in his administration of pain/pleasure, but his boundaries seemed to be rock-solid.

Tony Dent was the perfect complement to the darker edge that was Whiteside's method of operation. Tony was a Dom, but he preferred to gain compliance with sugar rather than discipline. Every sub at the club who had spent any time at all with Tony loved him, and Logan had been amazed at how quickly the man could gain their total submission. Tony didn't make any secret of the fact he'd love to find a sub of his own and settle down, but the only times he'd been edging toward that, the women had rejected him once they discovered his left leg was a prototype prosthesis.

The last time a sub had made disparaging remarks about Tony's condition, Ian had marched the very naked young woman up to his office where he lectured her on the finer points of respect. He'd pointed out to her there was no place in his club for anyone who did not hold the service and sacrifice of America's military members in the highest regard. He wrote her a check for the prorated balance of her membership and sent her on her way. When he reentered the club's main room, he'd been greeted by a standing ovation—it was the only time Logan could remember seeing Ian McGregor blush.

Tonight, Tony's leathers covered both legs, but the

open flap in the front showed his very erect penis as it was disappearing into Lizzy's pussy. Tony was sitting on an armless chair holding Lizzy up with his arms under her upper thighs. Lizzy's hands were on Tony's shoulders, and she was helping lift herself up in time with Tony's commands.

"Sweet Lizzy, your body is a treat, and I'm going to miss your wit and smile when you move. Now, are you ready for Master Don?"

Lizzy's voice was barely audible over the speakers, telling Logan she was probably already in subspace. He could see the faint lines on her back from Don's single tail and knew the men would have prepared her well for their performance. Lizzy's airy "yes" had Tony pulling her against his chest and kissing her with what appeared to be a smoldering intensity that reminded Logan of the kiss he'd shared with Abby down at the bar.

Logan moved behind Abby and pulled her back against his chest. Cupping one breast in his large hand, he gently squeezed the tight nipple between his fingers, her gasp sending his blood rushing south.

"Tell me what you see, baby."

"Lizzy is already in that endorphin-drenched state you call subspace, isn't she? I can see lines on her back, but they don't appear to be causing her any pain."

Logan was damned impressed Abby had even noticed the lines because they were extremely faint, and considering everything else happening, it wasn't a detail most people would notice first. But then Abby Garrett wasn't most people—not by a long shot.

"You're right, she is in subspace, and Don Whiteside is an expert with a single tail whip. Every warm brush to sizzling sting would have been planned for Lizzy's benefit.

By the time there was any pain at all, her body would have had trouble knowing where the line between the two opposite sensations was drawn. That is why it is important for the Dom to be well trained and know the sub he is working with. Doms must be able to recognize when his or her sub has had enough, especially if the submissive can no longer make the call."

When he felt her stiffen and shudder, he said, "The dance of a single tail is not for every submissive, Abby, but it's something Lizzy enjoys, so it was probably a going away gift for her."

Logan slid his free hand under her dress and slowly drew his fingers through the folds of her pussy. It didn't surprise him she wasn't as wet as she had been downstairs, considering her reaction. But he was pleased when he felt her begin to relax after he explained the marks on Lizzy's back. When Don stepped up behind Lizzy and started preparing her ass by pressing his well-lubed fingers inside her back passage, Abby's pussy flooded his fingers with her sweet cream, and Logan wanted to shout out his gratitude to the Universe for the gift of Abby Garrett.

"Do you see how he is preparing her to take him in the most intimate way? How he is making sure those delicate tissues are lubed and stretched, so they don't tear? The only pain they want her to feel is the kind that sears with pleasure.

"Watch closely how firmly Master Tony holds her as Master Don presses his cock in deep. They don't want her to push back before her body is truly ready. She could easily hurt herself even though that is what her mind is convinced it wants right at the moment. Her safety and well-being are their top priority, just as your care will always be ours."

Seeing Lizzy's total submission to their friends was sending Logan's arousal into orbit because, in a way, she was submitting to him and Kalen as well. Lizzy was often a handful as a sub, and that was the reason she still hadn't found a Dom willing to claim her long-term. Although Logan had the feeling the truth was closer to Lizzy hadn't found a Dom she felt was worthy of claiming her yet. He hoped if they opened a club in Texas, they could help her find what she was looking for.

ABBY'S MIND WAS whirling with everything she'd seen during their quick tour of the club. The images and sounds were being layered one atop the next until she'd already been battling her own release during the last two scenes they'd stopped to watch. But now... watching Lizzy between the two dark Doms, Abby felt like she was being catapulted toward the point of no return. Lizzy's Cajun accent was starting to surface in bits and pieces, and Abby remembered Jace telling her Lizzy and Ethan Jantz were cousins, so it made sense they'd have similar speech patterns. She'd found it interesting they'd both chosen to work for Uncle Sam in ways that served and protected our nation's people.

Logan's words against her ear were pure audible seduction. His voice had to be a gift from God himself, and she smiled to herself, then thought about how grateful the world should be he used this skill for good and not evil. The thought of him being an angel in disguise forced her to bite the inside of her mouth to keep her smile from bubbling up from the depths of her heart. If he was in disguise, it was a mighty fine one that was for darned sure.

Abby was no one's fool, she knew why they'd brought her to watch this scene, and she appreciated their efforts to make sure she understood exactly what they expected of her. But the sight of Don Whiteside pressing the deep purple head of his cock into Lizzy's nether hole was almost more than she could watch without coming herself. *Damn, let's go already. I want to be between you two right now.*

When Kalen had set her on the bar downstairs and bared her to the entire room, Abby had almost come on the spot. She hadn't had any idea being watched would be such a huge turn-on, but her body had given her away in a New York minute. She hadn't moved her eyes from Kalen's, but in her peripheral vision, she'd seen two Dom's order their subs to their knees for impromptu blow jobs as they'd watched Kalen play with her, and knowing she'd had such a profound effect on them turned her on more than she wanted to admit.

Logan's fingers were trailing through her soaking folds, circling her needy clit but weren't applying even the smallest bit of pressure it would take to send her over. "Please, Master. Please, let me come." Just as she spoke the words, she felt her knees start to shake.

"Hold it back, baby. We aren't finished watching Lizzy get double fucked yet." His crude words jacked her arousal even higher.

I sure didn't need that... I'm barely holding on the way it is. When the two men starting thrusting in and out of Lizzy in perfectly choreographed strokes, so one of them was always buried deep inside of her, Abby saw Lizzy begin to tremble as if the quaking had begun at her core, making the vibrations race to the surface for release. Lizzy's head leaned back, and Abby was treated to the most beautiful scream she'd ever heard. The sound was pure sexual release, and its effect on both of Doms was immediate. They set up a fast, but perfectly timed rhythm for another full minute before they both slammed their cocks deep and shouted as their own releases claimed them.

Just as the two men came, Logan pinched her clit, the vibe in her ass lit her up like the Christmas tree in Rockefeller Center, and Logan's command, "Come for us, baby" wasn't even fully spoken yet when she felt herself being flung out into space. The entire world exploded into blinding streaks of neon color. Abby was certain many of the shades didn't even actually exist, but she was happy to let her mind dismiss the criticism as creative latitude.

Before she realized what had happened, she was being carried through a door she hadn't even noticed and quickly down the hall to their apartment. Logan easily shifted her, so her legs were wrapped around his waist and pushed her down onto his cock the minute they were through the bedroom door. *Cripes. When did he open his pants?* She'd been so lost in the after-effects of her orgasm, she hadn't even noticed him freeing his erection from the dark jeans he'd been wearing. The urgent feeling of him pushing through her wet folds and the heat from stretching the sensitive walls of her vagina was enough to send her right back over.

"Very pretty, baby. Goddamn, I love watching you come—and holding you close while you let go is even better." He started pumping in as deep as the position allowed, then tilted his hips forward, forcing her to lean backward. Abby found herself up against Kalen's bare chest and sighed.

Kalen pushed her back up, just enough to pull her dress over her head, then pulled her roughly back again his chest, captured both of her breasts in his hands, rolling her nipples tightly between his fingers. When he tugged them hard enough to make her gasp, she felt electricity trace its way from her nipples to her sex, and she tumbled head over heels into bliss again.

It was long minutes before Abby resurfaced and realized Kalen was now holding her and from the smile on his face, he was the one flexing his cock inside her.

"Welcome back, love. That was quite the ride, wasn't it? You respond so beautifully to just a bit of pain, and that pleases both of your Masters more than we can tell you. Neither of us is a sadist, but the joy of the power exchange is sweeter for us when we can watch your body take a small bite of pain and turn it into pure pleasure."

Abby felt like she was just waking up, and her mind still wasn't all the way *engaged* yet. She felt herself blinking in her attempt to focus, and that's when she felt Logan behind her and the cool lube he was drizzling down the crack of her ass, then massaging into the outer rim of her anus. *When did they take out the plug?*

Logan leaned down and licked just behind her ear, and she felt herself shudder at the intimacy of the act.

"I took it out while you were still floating back to earth, baby. And I'm damned happy we sent you high enough, you weren't aware it happened. That level of orgasm takes some women years to be able to attain and watching you go there so easily under our hands is a huge gift."

Well, she couldn't really speak for them, but it had most certainly been fine and fucking dandy from her side of things.

Chapter 21

SINKING HIS COCK deep inside Abby while she'd still been in the midst of a mind-blowing orgasm had been without any doubt the most erotic moment of Kalen's life. She'd known on a base level when he'd buried himself in her because she'd called out his name as she'd splintered apart in another mind-numbing release. Holding her close as she came back to earth and seeing the sated look in her eyes as she tried to focus on his face filled him with a sense of love and satisfaction he'd never known before.

Kalen listened as Logan explained he'd removed the plug while she'd been floating, and he knew it was unlikely she caught more than bits and pieces of what her other Master was saying. No doubt Logan also knew she wasn't tracking full-on either, but this was exactly where they wanted her right now. The important thing would be holding her securely enough against him, so she wouldn't buck back against Logan and hurt herself. Logan met his eyes and nodded, so Kalen knew he was ready to start. Kalen tightened his arms around her.

"Are you ready to become ours, Abby? This is a very significant moment in our lives as a ménage family." He had deliberately used the word "family" because that was exactly how he saw the three of them. Kalen also knew it would have meaning for her because she had grown up in a family, not unlike the one he and Logan wanted to create with her. He saw her eyes fill with tears, and when she whispered her assent, he knew his words had gone to her heart, exactly as he had intended them to.

"I love you, Abigail. I have loved you for a very long time." He sealed his lips over hers and drank in the sweet taste that was Abby Garrett.

Tracing her lips with his tongue, he took full advantage of her gasp as Logan started pushing in and out in slow movements Kalen was just beginning to feel through the thin membrane separating his and Logan's positions inside the sweet woman they were claiming. Just as they'd expected, Abby seemed to sink quickly into the sensations of them surrounding her, and he felt her body tense just a split second before she would have thrust back if Kalen hadn't held her so securely.

"No, Abigail. Don't move. Hold still and let Master Logan take what is his. His moves are deliberately slow, so your body has time to stretch enough to accommodate him."

"Now... please, do it now. I can't wait. It's too much and not enough at the same time. My mind is trying to be obedient, but my body wants more... a *lot* more." Abby's voice had the edge of desperation that was music to every Dom's ears. She was already fluttering around his cock, and her breathing was little more than shallow panting. Kalen heard Logan take several deep breaths and knew his friend was trying to hold off the urge to shove in until he was balls deep in her ass.

"Fuck me. She is so tight. Baby, you hold my heart in the palm of your hand. I love you to the depths of my soul, but I'm riding a fine edge here, and if you don't stop squeezing me, I'm going to fuck you into oblivion and beyond."

Kalen felt Abby's entire body start to shake, then her muscles locked down on him like a wet velvet fist. Kalen watched Logan lean forward, bite down on her shoulder, and whisper, "Come for us, baby." She'd already been on the verge of coming, but his words seemed to amp up her release. Kalen was teetering on the edge as well, and every contraction, every groan, and every whimper was pushing him closer. Immediately, he and Logan started alternating their thrusts, so one of them was deep inside Abby at all times.

"I'm going to come, love, and when I do, I want you to feel every splash of seed as it bathes your womb's opening." Logan shouted Abby's name and Kalen could feel the pulses of his release and the aftershocks of Abby's orgasm. The combination of the two was all it took to launch him into a release that literally stole his breath. He heard himself shout her name but wouldn't have recognized his own voice if he hadn't felt the strain of his vocal chords. By the time his cock stopped shooting hot pulses of his seed deep into the love of his life, Kalen felt like his balls had been turned inside out.

He finally realized Abby was fighting for every breath because he still had his arms wrapped around her in a vise-like grip—hell, it was a miracle he hadn't broken a couple of her ribs.

"Oh, love, I'm so sorry. Are you alright? I didn't crush you, did I?" Kalen caught her face between his palms and lifted it, so he could see into her eyes and felt as if someone had dropped an anvil on his chest when he saw she was crying.

"No, I am fine, but I can breathe easier now." She smiled weakly through her tears.

"Then why are you crying? Abigail, if I've hurt you, I'll never forgive myself." Kalen was nearing panic, thinking he'd hurt the most important person in his world. Abby's smile brightened, thawing the fear that had nearly frozen him in place and relief swept through his entire body.

"It was just so amazing... I don't even know how to describe it. To hear you both say you love me when I love you so much... well, it just overwhelmed me a little." She gasped, then groaned as Logan pulled out of her, and he heard his friend speak to her quietly about staying put. Honestly, Kalen was so lost in her words and his own overwhelming sense of relief at finding out he hadn't hurt her, he was having trouble focusing on anything else.

When his cock finally slipped from her warmth, Kalen felt a surge of primal satisfaction at the feeling of their combined releases running out of her and coating their thighs.

After cleaning up, he and Logan settled Abby between them, and he was relieved to see her sleeping before they were able to put out the lights.

"She has been stealing pieces of my heart since I met her and damned if she didn't take the last of it tonight. I want her to sleep a bit before we wake her up for round two and give her our gift."

"I agree. It humbles me to realize how everything that matters to me now centers entirely around the happiness and safety of this woman." Logan's words were true of him as well, and it was indeed very humbling to see how quickly life could change. Something about that thought sent a spike of unease through Kalen. Tomorrow was going to be a test of their trust in Abby's ability to take care of herself, and despite the fact she'd done a fine job of it for years, it was setting off every single internal alarm he possessed. He'd dropped into war zones amid hostile enemy troops more often than he cared to remember, and he'd never been as nervous about any of those ops as he was about Abby using herself as bait tomorrow night.

ABBY WAS SLOWLY coming awake, shivering involuntarily as her mind kicked into gear enough to realize she was no longer snuggled securely between Kalen and Logan. For just a second, she flashed back to waking up in the trunk of a car after her kidnapping. Stiffening her back and gasping for air, Abby tried to focus her mind and immediately felt soothing hands gliding up and down her arms. Taking a deep breath, she knew the touch was Kalen's by the soft sandalwood scent of his cologne.

"Easy, love. You're safe and right where we want you." Abby noted she was standing in front of a large soft pillow. When she moved her focus back to the men standing in front of her, they helped her kneel. The smooth fabric under her knees felt cool to the touch, and she was surprised at how well it cushioned her position. The lights were still off, but the soft golden flickering light of candles danced over nearby stone walls, creating a visual that was erotic and romantic at the same time.

Her mind stumbled over the fact the walls had turned to stone, but the smell of both Logan and Kalen surrounding her was so intoxicating, her mind was quieted by the strength of her body's reaction to them. Her nipples peaked, and her pussy flooded with moisture—everything in her wanted to submit herself to them and become theirs. After she'd taken a couple of deep breaths, she felt Logan's chest press against her back, and his warm breath was a warm summer's breeze kissing her neck from over her shoulder.

"Baby, we have something very important to ask you. Do you know what a collar is in BDSM circles? Did all your research teach you what a deep commitment it represents?" Abby's mind was jolted into fully functioning by Logan's words, and heaven knew, she was fully awake now.

"Yes, I did read about collars. Everything I read indicated they represent a deeper commitment than marriage even though they aren't legally recognized unions. They seem to be deeply honored and highly respected by everyone involved in the lifestyle." She actually knew quite a lot more but didn't know exactly how much they wanted to hear her recite. She often bored her family and friends to distraction with her ability to list facts and statistics in excruciating detail.

"Baby, there isn't a thing about you that bores either of us."

Abby felt cool metal slide over her shoulder and knew in an instant what it had to be, and her heart stuttered at the enormity of this moment. Kalen's smile went right to her soul and brought a sense of peace she had always felt was just out of her grasp.

"I see the recognition in your expressive eyes, love. We've created a one of a kind collar for you, and we would be honored if you would accept it as a sign of our deep commitment to you. But first, we want you to understand exactly what we're giving you, and what we'll expect in return."

Abby noted the pillow she knelt on rested on a huge boulder flattened on the top like the ones at her family's ranch in Texas. She flicked her gaze around and saw she was in one of the more secluded stage areas of the club. Judging by how few people were watching, she assumed it was late, probably not long before the club's three a.m. closing time. Logan's smile was sweet, but his eyes were full of heat.

"Do you know why we've brought you into the club, baby?" When she only shook her head, Logan merely raised a brow.

"No, I don't know why I'm here or even how I got here, actually." She shuddered at the thought she had been sleeping so soundly, she hadn't even realized they'd moved her. If she let her guard down like that tomorrow, she could easily find herself in a major jam. Logan grasped her chin between his fingers and brought her focus to his face.

"Baby, we want your focus on *this moment*, do you understand?"

Oh yeah, she read that loud and clear. *Stop your damned spacey little trips into la-la land, Abby.*

"Yes, Sir, I understand. I'm sorry. I'm just a bit unnerved by the fact I slept through you moving me." She felt her eyes fill with tears but refused to let them fall. "I've been trying to be so careful for so long, and I haven't slept that soundly for months. The idea I could have woken up in the back of a car again scares me." Her conscious mind knew she'd been safe, but she suspected it was going to take a while for her subconscious to catch up.

"I'm sorry, baby. Neither of us realized it would have that effect on you, or we would have done this differently."

She could see the regret in his eyes and felt a pang of guilt for putting it there, but she really had been frightened so in the end, she was glad she'd been honest.

"We need you to always be honest with us. If something unsettles you, we need to know. As a matter of fact, we're going to demand to know about anything that concerns you."

Logan's words were caring, but there was an underlying band of steel in them Abby didn't miss. She'd grown up with two fathers who were both Doms, and she knew they'd both been far angrier at both her and her mother for *not* sharing something that upset them than they had ever been for anything either of them had actually done.

Her older brother had only been mad at her once that she could remember, and that had been the time a boy in junior high school had cornered her outside the school one night while she'd waited on her ride. The kid had scared her with his taunts about her family and threatened her if she told anyone, so she'd kept quiet. But Jace had known the minute she got home something was wrong, and when she had refused to answer his questions, he'd been beyond pissed.

It had been Abby's mom who had finally gotten Jace calmed down enough to see he was causing as much damage as whoever had scared her. Jace had been a senior and getting ready to leave for the Navy in a few weeks, and Abby hadn't wanted him to do anything that would jeopardize him realizing his dream. He'd eventually convinced her he would be rational and had calmly listened to her story. She'd appreciated him teaching her several self-defense moves and buying her a small can of pepper spray.

About a week before the end of the school year, the bully had shown up at school with two black eyes and a split lip. Abby never got Jace to admit to his part in it, but the fact the kid had been terrified to be anywhere near her had been all the proof she'd needed. Taking a deep breath,

Abby realized she'd been lost in her memories, and both of her Doms were looking at her with a combination of amusement and frustration.

"Love, someday we really are going to have you tell us all about your little mental jaunts into oblivion, but right now, we want to talk to you about the significance of a collar and the two options we have tonight. We won't always give you the opportunity to have input when we're planning a scene—actually, we will rarely give you that chance. But tonight may well be the most important moment in the relationship we plan to build with you, and we want you to be completely on-board with the way it plays out."

Kalen had stopped talking, but he continued to softly stroke the sides of her cheeks with his thumbs. His touch was both soothing and helping to bring her focus back to him with each pass.

How do they know? Do they understand how every small detail of their care carves itself into my heart? That my love and trust grow with every look and caress?

Chapter 22

KALEN WATCHED EVERY movement Abby made, because no matter how small or insignificant they might seem to someone else, each one had meaning. As a former Special Forces soldier who was also a Dom, he considered himself an expert in reading and interpreting the meaning of a person's body language. Kalen found it interesting that even the ancient philosophers made reference to the importance of watching the "windows of the soul," and Abby's dark eyes spoke as clearly as any he'd ever seen.

One of the most remarkable things about the incredible woman kneeling in front of him was, in part, the fact she considered herself so ordinary. Kalen was letting her settle a bit as he swept his thumbs over her cheekbones, and he wondered if it wasn't actually more for his own sake than for hers. It gave him a tremendous amount of satisfaction to know she was so responsive to both his and Logan's touch. When he saw her muscles finally lose most of their tension, he knew she was where he needed her to be and gave her a smile he knew she'd understand. He'd been told by more than one sub his voice was seductive magic, and he planned to take full advantage of it now.

"Abby, in order to do your collaring in the club, we have to meet certain requirements. One of those is Ian's personal blessing which we have obtained. Another is it must be done during the regular operating hours of the club, and we're within that time, but without a whole lot to spare. The third is that there must be at least one single tail whip strip for each person involved in the relationship, so in our case, that is three." He felt her start to shake and watched as her eyes started chasing around the room as if looking for an escape.

He firmed his hands along her face, refocusing her attention on him. "Abigail, look at me and only at me." When she did, he smiled at her, "Stay with me, love. Do you trust that Master Logan and I will never hurt you?"

The fear that had been in her eyes started to abate, but he could see she wasn't fully cognizant of what he was asking her. He just waited, knowing she would work it out in her mind quickly enough. She finally seemed to come back to center and nodded.

"Yes, sir. I have entrusted you both with my heart, so it seems perfectly reasonable to give you my body as well." Her words were perfect, and for just a moment, he wanted nothing more than to scoop her up and take her right back upstairs to bed.

"Your trust is our most treasured possession, love. Never forget how much we adore you." He sealed his lips over hers and poured himself into the kiss, hoping it would show her the depth of his love even when words had eluded him.

Helping her to her feet and turning her into Logan's arms, so he could be behind her, was one of the hardest things Kalen had ever done. He and Logan had agreed on a slight variation of the position ordinarily used, and Ian had been in full agreement. There was a temporary collar they could have used if she had been too frightened to take the lashes, but it didn't have the advanced electronics of the one they'd commissioned for her, and it wouldn't have had the same significance for any of them.

Picking up the single tail he'd always enjoyed using didn't give him the same rush tonight. Kalen knew the feeling of fulfillment he usually got from showing a sub how the line between pain and pleasure could be blurred would be forever eclipsed by the deep satisfaction he got from seeing Abby give herself so freely to both him and Logan.

LOGAN KISSED ABBY until they were both falling over the edge into need that only had one cure. He was running his hands up and down her bare back, lightly scoring the skin with his fingernails, bringing the blood to the surface. Kalen would pull the lashes, but they still needed there to be marking in order to satisfy some of the more hardline players who were watching with avid interest.

Abby probably hadn't given any thought to the fact she was naked in the club. While she'd knelt, her knees had been spread wide, and her pretty, pink pussy had been on display for anyone wandering by to see. He pulled back and licked her lips slowly so her mind wasn't tossed starkly in out of the sea of lust he'd worked so hard to create.

"Baby, we are going to do this a bit differently than most of these ceremonies. Master Kalen is much more experienced with the whip in his hand than I am, so he'll be giving you all three marks. Instead of tying you to the St. Andrew's cross as is customary, you'll be leaning against me while I hold you against my chest. What this means is you must be absolutely still and let me control your position." When he saw the fear in her eyes and unshed tears fill them, his heart nearly melted. "Trust, Abby. It's only the first of many things we want from you, but it is the most important."

He ran his fingers through her pussy lips and found there was very little moisture there and wasn't surprised because her battle with fear was stealing all her concentration. Pulling her against him, he whispered, "You are going to hear a couple of practice cracks of the whip because Master Kalen wants his arm warmed up, and he'll be checking the distance to make sure you only feel exactly what he wants you to feel."

Logan swept her long hair over her shoulder, baring her back and ass to Kalen. Sending up a silent prayer they'd made the right decision by not securing her to a cross, Logan encircled both of her wrists and stretched her arms wide and pulled them slightly forward, so she was held firmly against his chest. When Kalen cracked the leather on first one side of Abby's small back, then the other, Logan felt her stiffen and gasp. He kissed the top of her head and tightened his hold on her wrists.

"Those two marks mean you belong to us, baby." Logan knew the first lash had landed perfectly, and Abby's jump had been more in surprise than pain. "Every beat of your heart is ours to share." The second lash had brought about the sweetest moan he'd ever heard. Logan wanted to crush her in his arms and let her know just how lovely that small sound, signaling her submission and arousal, was to his ears.

It was only when he saw Kalen make eye contact with someone behind him, Logan realized Ian was standing just behind his right arm. He smiled to himself because he knew Ian wasn't going to leave a single thing to chance when it came to Abby, and that filled him with a new level of respect and appreciation for the man. Kalen shifted his position because the last lash mark would cross two she'd already received. Logan was sure the first two marks were perfectly parallel and diagonally placed across her golden tan-colored skin.

The whistle of the whip moving through the air signaled the last lash a split second before he felt Abby start to arch forward so her back was now closer than Kalen would have calculated it to be. Logan nearly lost his mind in fear because he'd seen the damage a single tail could do to flesh.

Even the smallest movement on her part could make the difference between the line of quickly extinguishing fire and a slice that would require immediate medical attention. Logan resisted the urge to inhale sharply, which would have filled his lungs and pushed her that much closer to the whip. Instead, his instinct to protect and shelter had him pulling her back from the danger just enough to prevent her from being seriously hurt, but not enough to keep her from feeling the very real bite of a single-tail without the benefit of the sweet build-up of endorphins. Logan knew her scream would echo through his nightmares for years to come.

THE INSTANT HIS wrist snapped, Kalen realized Abby had moved ever so slightly. Kalen saw the look of panic so clearly written in Logan's expression and heard Abby's scream at almost the exact same moment. The whip dropped from his hand, and if he never touched it again, it would be fine by him. A thousand things they could have done differently raced through his mind and not one of them changed the deep red welt already forming over Abby's delicate skin. Kalen was frozen in place. No matter how much he willed his feet to move, they seemed to be nailed to the floor.

Logan was consoling their sobbing woman, and Kalen was standing across the small stage as if he was made of stone. He didn't doubt there were people in the room who would interpret his distance and lack of response as further evidence he was a cold bastard he was often accused of being. Oddly enough, it was Callie's sweet voice and the soft touch of her warm fingers on his arm that jolted him out of his paralysis. "She needs you," was all his sweet friend said, but it was enough. He nodded and rushed to Abby's side.

Ian was already lightly rubbing arnica gel into the angry mark, and Abby's gasp at the cool gel was nearly covered by the quiet sobs threatening to break his heart. When she felt his hand on her, she didn't flinch away as he'd feared she might, but her words nearly brought him to his knees.

"I'm sorry, Master Kalen. I know I wasn't supposed to move. Please don't be angry."

Angry? With her? Is she fucking serious? Oh, hell yes, he was angry all right—angry at himself and Logan for thinking they could do this in a nonconventional way so she'd feel more comfortable. Their attempt to make things "better" had made it a nightmare for her. And now, she thinks this disaster is *her* fault? Un-fucking-believable.

"Love, you are the only one I am not angry with." He took her into his arms and just held her for long moments. "I'm so sorry. Fifty years from now, I'll still hear your scream echo in my mind. Hurting the woman I treasure above everything else felt like someone shoving a dull butter knife into my heart." He moved his hands to each side of her face and kissed away her tears. He just stood for long moments looking into her eyes—searching for some sign her feelings for him hadn't dimmed. What he saw was pure love that ran soul deep, and even though he didn't feel worthy of it at this moment, he wasn't about to let it go.

"Come on love, let's get you home." Kalen started to lead her from the stage, but she stood still and blinked up at him.

"You aren't going to do it now? Because I messed up, right?" Huge round, glistening teardrops raced down her cheeks again, and he swore he could hear her heart-shattering. In an instant, he knew she'd interpreted his move to get her home so they could comfort and care for her as a rejection. *She thinks we aren't going to collar her because she moved and got hurt. Could we fuck this up any worse?*

Logan turned her, so she faced him. "Baby, we just wanted to take care of you, but if you want to finish the ceremony, we're not going to turn away from the best thing that has ever happened to either of us." She nodded her head, then remembered she needed to verbalize her answers.

"Yes, I want that more than anything. I might not be the best submissive around, but I love you more than life itself, and I'm loyal to the very depths of my soul. You already know what a pain in the ass I can be sometimes, so I don't think you are flying into this blind." Kalen was relieved beyond measure to see the Abby he'd fallen in love with resurfacing so quickly and shining through the tears.

"Love, you will probably never be the perfect sub, and we wouldn't change that for the world." Kalen stepped forward and gave her a smile he hoped she knew came from his heart. "You are the most amazing woman I've ever known and waiting for you has seemed interminable, but there hasn't been a single moment either Logan or I thought it wasn't worth it. Before we present you with the collar we had made for you, Master Logan and I both want to tell you exactly what it means to us."

LOGAN STROKED HIS fingers down the sides of her face with a touch so slow and sensuous, it was almost foreplay, and he prayed the throbbing across her back would be long forgotten by the time his words washed through her soul.

"There will never be a moment when your safety and happiness are not our priority. There will probably be many moments when you vehemently disagree with us about what constitutes *safe*, but I want you to always remember our love for you will always be paramount. In those moments when you want to scream in frustration because you feel one or likely both of us are being unreasonable, keep in your heart we love you with an intensity that may often make us err on the side of the angels."

He knew Abby would recognize the expression because Logan knew it was one of her mother's favorites, and he wanted her to know he'd always been listening. He also wanted her to know he'd seen the care her fathers had always shown her and her mother, and he and Kalen would do no less. Logan took a deep breath, trying to stay the emotion swelling within him and watched as Kalen moved closer. His best friend brought her attention to him by running his hand down her arm and encircling her wrist before slowly turning her to face him.

"Love, there is only one thing we won't do for you. We'll never let you put yourself in harm's way unless we are right there beside you. We'll be your biggest support-ers, your knights in shining armor, and your sounding board in the middle of the night when self-doubt or fear hide in the shadows. But we won't be negligent in our care for you—ever. The fates have entrusted you to us, and we'll protect you with everything we have."

True to form, Kalen's words had been short and sweet. Logan remembered Abby asking Kalen once why he didn't say much. He'd looked at her with thoughtful sincerity and said, "Truth never requires a lot of words." Not long ago, Abby told them she had never forgotten those words, and as she'd grown, both personally and professionally, she'd seen just how significant his answer had been.

"KNEEL, ABIGAIL." KALEN'S words had sounded gruff, but Abby could see he was as affected by the moment as she was. She knelt in front of them and felt the cool metal slide over her skin as it circled the base of her throat, but then it was gone. Kalen was holding the beautiful choker in his open hands in front of her, the diamonds and rubies sparkling in the dim lights from the club's wall sconces. *If it shines like that in this light, it's going to blind people when the sunlight hits it.*

When she looked back up at their faces, she saw they were smiling. Logan's voice was just this side of teasing,

"Do you like it, baby? We worked with a very special team to design it just for you."

"Yes, Sir, it's stunning. But… umm, what do you mean by a *team*?"

"There are a number of special features to this collar, Abigail. First, because of the metals used and the tamper-proof lock, let us assure you, no one is ever going to take what is yours alone. Master Logan and I will have the only keys on our persons at all times. It also features the latest technology from Masters Ian and Mitch. Their wives will be getting their own, but not until after this is gracing your lovely neck.

"Baby, before we snap this collar into place, we need to know if you understand and agree to everything we've said to you. Safe, sane, and consensual are more than just politically correct gibberish. Those three words will be the guiding tenants of every scene we'll ever do with you. And Abby, this is only the first step of the lifelong commitment we're asking you to make."

Suddenly, Abby realized her heart was beating like some drug-crazed squirrel had seized hold of the controls. She started seeing dots in front of her eyes before she heard Kalen's sharp command.

"Abigail, breathe." When she focused, they were both kneeling in front of her, so they were all face to face. She took several deep breaths and looked into their eyes and knew from their worried expressions, they had both misinterpreted her panic.

"You want to marry me? Is that what you are saying?"

Kalen's usually serene expression turned to fire in an instant. "Abigail, be very careful how you proceed with this line of questioning because it sounds suspiciously like you find that hard to believe."

"Well, yeah. I'm actually kind of stunned to tell you the truth."

"Baby, you better explain that comment—quickly."

Oh, brother, now she'd riled up both her Doms, and she could see Ian standing off to the side with his brow raised in question. *Real bright move, Miss Genius IQ. Hell, you're three for three. Why can't you keep your mouth shut? Good grief Gertie, I'm a dip sometimes. Holy shit, did they just growl at me?*

"Okay, okay, hang on to your hats, cowboys, don't get your chaps up your ass, geez." The instant the words left her mouth, Abby knew she'd messed up. Hell, the scowls were giving her now could peel paint off a battleship. *Oh, mercy.*

Chapter 23

L OGAN WASN'T SHOCKED by *what* Abby had said, hell, he'd visited the Garretts' ranch in Texas often enough have heard most of their colloquial slang. But the fact that she *had* said it, in this setting, shocked the hell out of him— it also told him just how rattled she'd been by their back-handed proposal. *Fucking hell.* That's when it hit him, they hadn't actually proposed to her. They'd just assumed she would know what they expected. *Oh yeah, we're a couple of real romantic bastards. Jesus, Joseph, and Mary, it's a wonder she didn't tell us both just where to jump.*

It didn't matter at this point she might have a legiti-mate complaint with their lack of finesse, it was the fact she'd dared to be flip while they were clearly in a scene, in the club, on a stage in front of the owner—how it could have been worse, Logan didn't even want to consider. Kalen had already led Abby over to a nearby armless chair and sat in it, so the only way he had of slowing this down was to speak up—quickly. Walking up to them, Logan turned her to face him.

"Abby, I understand we didn't handle that well. Okay, that may be an understatement, but you are so incredibly bright, it is easy to assume you 'already know' something when that clearly was not the case here. But that being said, your response was way over the line." He kissed her on the forehead and turned her back to Kalen before speaking over her shoulder. "Take your punishment with the grace and dignity you bring to everything else you do, then we'll continue."

In Logan's mind, this entire evening had been a cluster fuck of Biblical proportions. And now, all he could see in his mind's eye was a steam engine barreling down on a fog-enshrouded bridge spanning a deep canyon. The engineer going full-steam ahead in a misguided attempt to make up for lost time and blissfully unaware of the fact the bridge was missing a large section of track right over the deepest section of the river running at flood stage at the bottom of the rock-lined canyon.

He'd been on missions like this—where one disaster spawned the next and so on until the entire plan was completely unrecognizable. Sighing, he stepped back and watched Kalen pull Abby over his lap, so her bare ass was peaked and in position for the spanking that was to come. Logan wasn't sure what had snapped inside of Kalen, but evidently, his words had finally made it through the cloud of anger that had surrounded his friend. Kalen looked up at Logan and nodded as if saying "message received" before leaning down and speaking to Abby.

"Love, I don't want to punish you, but you've left me no choice. That flippant comment during any scene would have gotten you a punishment, but to be so crass during your collaring and on stage in front of the owner of the club is unforgivable. Because Master Logan and I both feel we share some responsibility for your confusion, you're only being punished for the attitude, not for your previous remarks which I am certain were self-depreciating."

All the time he'd been speaking to her, he'd been running his fingers over the smooth lips of her bare pussy, teasing her with his touch, trying to get her back in the right mindset before his palm lit up her ass like the Fourth of July. He was pleased to feel her pussy becoming moist at his touch despite the fact a punishment was coming her way.

"You will get ten swats from my hand and ten more from Master Logan. When we are finished, you will kneel and apologize to everyone watching, particularly to Master Ian for your disrespect. Then we'll continue with your collaring if you still want to belong to Master Logan and me."

Logan heard her sniff and knew she was already crying, but hearing it made him feel as if his heart was being squeezed in a vise.

Kalen continued, "Because this is your first punishment in the club, you won't need to count the swats out loud. Oh, and you aren't allowed to come, Abigail, don't forget that."

Abby's thoughts raced through Logan's mind as surely as if she'd spoken them aloud, *"Is he joking? He's going to beat me, and he thinks I'm going to come? Not fucking likely."* Logan managed to not laugh because he fully intended to make her come during his ten swats. He wanted to prove to her they knew her needs better than she did, but he also wanted to make sure the punishment ended on a note that wasn't going to add to the disaster this night had become.

Hoping Kalen was going to take it easy on Abby and back off his swats turned out to be a pipe dream as the first several landed with resounding whacks, followed by gasps and sobs from their sweet woman. Glancing around him, Logan was frustrated to see several of the subs he and Kalen had scened with smiling smugly. *Don't think this means we aren't keeping her because the opposite is true. She is being punished, so she understands her value and how her behavior reflects her feelings of security and self-worth. If we didn't love her, we'd just let her go—like we did you.*

By the time Kalen had finished his ten spanks, Abby's ass was fire engine red, and it was easy to see the tissues below the skin were swelling in response to the pounding her skin had taken. Logan didn't doubt for a second it was extremely sore, and he knew he was going to have to be very careful because there was already evidence of deep tissue bruising.

He saw Gage Hughes standing to the side, his jaw clenched and his mouth in a straight line. Logan took a deep breath and let it out slowly. He was glad Jace hadn't come down because that would have just been too much for Abby to deal with and humiliating her had never been the plan.

Kalen stood her up, and her knees buckled, but he caught her before she hit the floor. Logan glanced at Ian, and the instant their eyes met, Logan's decision was made. He stepped forward and spoke to Kalen.

"She's done, this stops now." Ordinarily, they always worked in tandem, but for the first time Logan could remember, Kalen had reacted in anger when deciding on a punishment, and there was too much at stake with Abby to add another mistake to tonight's cluster fuck.

ABBY'S ENTIRE BODY was so sensitized, she feared the slightest touch, and she would shatter. During her punishment, she'd been mad at herself and Kalen, but it was Logan's words that broke her heart into a million pieces.

She'd seen the angry looks on Ian's and Gage's faces, and knowing she'd disappointed them as well had been devastating. But when Logan stepped forward to say she was done, it had broken her. The room tilted on its axis and black dots swam in front of her. Sounds faded into the background, and all she could hear was the sound of blood rushing through her ears.

"No, please. Don't give up on me." Abby heard the words, but it barely registered she was actually speaking them out loud.

"Never." Logan's voice was strong, and his strength seemed to lend itself to her. "We'll re-negotiate the rest of your punishment later, baby. I think I can find an alternate method that will suit my needs better than continuing down this path." It was only then Abby realized Logan's firm grip around her biceps was the only thing holding her up... hell, her feet were barely touching the floor. She could feel Kalen's heat pressed against her throbbing back and ass and saw Ian and Gage standing on each side of her.

In a flash of insight, Abby realized they'd flanked her to protect her from the prying eyes of the club members whose morbid curiosity seemed to be feeding on the drama unfolding before them.

"Now that you seem to be back with us, baby, I'd like to finish this up and get you upstairs so we can take care of you. I'm going to set you down and help you kneel so you can apologize to Master Ian, then you have an important question to answer, little sub."

After she'd apologized to Ian, he lifted her chin with his cool fingers and kissed her forehead. "All is forgiven, sweetness. Please don't do this again, it broke my heart to see you hurting—both physically and emotionally." He stepped back and crossed his arms over his chest and simply nodded in what she assumed was a signal for Logan to continue.

Logan looked down at her and smiled, but she could see how tentative he was, and it flashed through her mind that she didn't ever remember seeing him as anything but self-assured. For the first time she could remember, she saw a hint of vulnerability in his eyes that made her love him even more.

Something deep in her soul responded to the knowledge he wasn't assuming she would simply throw herself into their arms. The choice was hers, and Logan didn't seem entirely sure how it was going to go. She felt her eyes fill with tears but tried to keep them from falling. She might have been successful too, but his words were so sweet she let the tears flow unchecked.

"Will you be ours, Abby? Will you wear our collar and accept all that it represents? As a part of that, we'll arrange a proper proposal, but be forewarned, it's coming, baby." He smiled at her and used his thumbs to wipe away the tears.

Kalen had stepped around her and picked up her hand. Turning it over gently, he placed a soft kiss in her palm. "Abigail, I've never hated a punishment more than that one. We'll talk it out at length, I promise you, but for now, I want you to be completely secure in my love for you. My desire to hold you and care for you until the end of time grows stronger with each beat of my heart."

Abby hadn't realized the beautiful choker was back in Logan's hands until he moved to place it around her neck.

"What is your decision, Abby? Because once the lock snaps in place, you are ours. We'll go to the ends of the earth to protect you. Our love for you and our loyalty to you will never be in question, but this decision is yours to make."

Taking a deep breath, she knew this was the easiest decision she'd ever make. "Yes, my heart already belongs to you... it has for a very long time. You make me a better person, and I hope there is never a single day you question the depth of the love filling my heart." She barely felt Logan's fingers move, but the snick of the locking mechanism on the choker was loud enough to bring cheers from everyone around them.

Abby felt herself being wrapped in a soft blanket, then she was in Kalen's arms. His expression was both filled with love and fierce possession. And even though they were responding politely to the congratulations being spoken all around them, neither Kalen nor Logan ever stopped walking toward the secured door leading to the apartments.

Almost of their own volition, Abby felt her fingers move to the choker and trace its smooth texture and cool stones as if it wasn't real somehow, and the whole evening would prove to be nothing but a sweet dream that would disappear like the mist over a hay meadow as the sun rises. The weight of the metal and jewels would serve as a constant reminder of the promises they'd all three made. The feel of it over her skin told her it was real, and so was her love for both of the men she'd just committed herself to.

Chapter 24

K ALEN HADN'T MISSED Abby's small hiss of pain as the soft subbie blanket had been wrapped around her back or her gasp as he'd scooped her up and her tender ass cheeks had slid over his forearm.

He'd known the minute Ian stepped back onto the stage, the club owner was sending a not-so-subtle message they needed to reevaluate how things were progressing, but for the first time in his life, Kalen had been so focused on a punishment, he'd lost sight of the real purpose of every BDSM scene—providing the submissive the best possible guidance and pleasure. When he considered those two goals, his performance tonight as a Dom had been a thundering failure.

How he'd managed to fuck up everything about the evening he wasn't sure, but he'd made one lousy decision after another. The fact Abby still agreed to be theirs was a huge testament to the strength of their previous relationship because he hadn't done a single thing tonight to earn her respect or her trust.

Walking directly to the master suite's spa bathtub, he set Abby on her feet and unwrapped her from the blanket like the precious gift she was while Logan started the water and added scented Epson salts. The sweet smell of lavender and sage filled the air, and its relaxing effect was almost

162

immediate as Kalen felt some of the tension drain out of his muscles and was relieved beyond measure to feel Abby relax against him.

The satisfaction of having her lean against him to rest her tear-stained cheek against the light dusting of hair over his pectorals was one of the most humbling moments of his life. Here was the love of his life, the most important person in the world, still willing to give him her love even though most people would have simply walked away. Settling her in the huge tub, so her sore bottom was between his legs, Kalen looked at Logan and hoped his friend knew how grateful he was that at least one of them had had the wisdom to call the scene off. Logan's subtle nod told Kalen he'd understood the unspoken thank you.

Kalen let the lavender and sage salts work their magic on Abby. When her eyelids started to droop, he smiled at Logan. "I think our little sub is about ready for a massage."

They'd quickly moved to the shower. He and Logan had washed Abby's long hair, then conditioned it before washing every luscious inch of her with soft tempting touches Kalen hoped were as arousing to her as they were to him.

"Love, your skin is so perfect. It is soft and supple under my fingertips. Watching the bubbles circle your nipples before sliding down your flat abdomen and disappearing between your legs makes my cock throb from wanting you. Feeling your pussy pulse around me is one of the greatest joys I've ever known." He knelt in front of her and buried his face at the junction of her thighs and inhaled.

Her soft sighs were barely audible over the soft sounds of the multiple water jets, but he'd heard them, anyway. Her pleading, "Please touch me" was all it took for him to move her legs apart enough, he could move the tip of his tongue around her clit in slow circles until she was gasping and writhing in Logan's arms. Kalen felt the muscles in her thighs begin to tremble and knew she was close, so he pulled back and smiled at her sweet sounds of frustration.

"Bed. Now." Those two words were all he managed to get out before they all moved out of the shower. They dried her quickly with soft pats of the towel, so they didn't aggravate the marks she'd gotten in the club. The welt from the whip's lash wasn't as swollen now, but it was still clearly visible even though the first two carefully placed lines were just a warm faded memory. But the cheeks of her ass needed tending to, and Kalen was going to make sure they massaged them with a cool gel that would wick the heat out and hopefully, abate the pain as well.

LOGAN HAD NEVER seen Kalen as hesitant with a woman or sub as he was acting with Abby since they'd returned to the apartment. He was sure his friend didn't realize the effect his changed behavior was having on their woman either. Kalen was reacting to Abby's tension which was being fed by Kalen acting so distant. The whole thing was a vicious cycle, and it didn't look like it was going to fix itself which left it up to him to broach the subject. While he helped Abby comb out the tangles in her long hair, he spoke up.

"Abby, in keeping with the openness we're going to demand of you, I want to talk to you about what happened tonight. I feel it is like the elephant standing in the corner no one wants to mention, but everyone sees clearly." He put his hands on her shoulders and turned her and walked her into the small sitting area of the bedroom. He pulled a silk robe over her shoulders and loosely tied it in front of her, making sure the gap provide enough of a view to satisfy the Dom in him.

Sitting her in the softest of the chairs, he pulled another chair close and settled in front of her. Grasping her hands in his, he smiled as she nervously bit her lower lip. He was easily able to grasp both of her wrists in one hand and raise the other one to use his thumb to pull her lip from between her teeth.

"That lip is ours to enjoy, baby." Her shy smile warmed his heart. "The only thing that went as we'd planned tonight is you are now wearing our collar. And while that is the most important part of what we'd planned, it doesn't change the fact both Kalen and I made several errors tonight." Logan smiled when Abby looked confused by his confession.

"Don't look so surprised, baby. Doms are human too, and we make mistakes, just like everyone else, but I've always believed the key to turning around mistakes is not making the same one more than once. That means we need to think back over the steps we took if we want to see clearly where things went south—or as my parents would say, when things went from sugar to shit." He was relieved to hear her giggle because even though they hadn't been raised near each other, he knew she would recognize the southern expression.

"I assure you there is going to be ample discussion about what went wrong this evening and how we can prevent any 'not-so-sweet' repeats. But right now, Kalen and I want to hurdle the biggest issues so we can celebrate our pride and overwhelming joy at seeing our collar laying against your lovely neck and the reassurance you have agreed to become ours *legally* as well. We'll leave the wedding details to you and your mom, but we aren't patient men, baby."

KALEN PULLED A chair up alongside Logan's, and Abby looked over at him for confirmation. She wondered why he hadn't joined them earlier and thought perhaps he'd changed his mind after her behavior earlier in the club.

"Are you sure, Kalen?" He looked stunned by her question, then understanding seemed to dawn in his eyes.

"Love, I wasn't over here sooner because I was setting up what I hope will be a very special surprise for you. Please don't misinterpret my late arrival in this conversation as not being fully on board with what Logan has just said." His smile warmed her from the inside, and when she started to turn around, he stopped her. "No, sweetheart. We want it to be a surprise, so let's finish this discussion before we move over to the bed."

"I'm sure my mom will want to host things just like she did for Jace, and I'm sure she'll be able to meet any time deadline, considering how quickly she pulled together everything for their celebration. But I really want you to be sure... well, because I'm kind of a hot mess sometimes, and I think we know how badly things went tonight. Sometimes, I think out loud, it's just how my mind works. I don't think I can change it, and quite frankly, I'm not sure I want to. I have to process information in certain ways, or things just don't work. And... well, I don't want to disappoint you again."

"Love, tonight was the most important one of my entire life, and I'm not sure I could have handled it any worse.

We won't allow you to be disrespectful to us or any Dom, particularly not while in the club, but that being said, my response was disproportionate for several reasons, including the fact you had already been injured by my hand. Honestly, even now when I think about it, I feel like I might actually be ill."

She could see the pain in his expression, but he seemed to pull strength up from deep inside, and it looked like he was going to forge on before he lost his nerve and retreated to the contemplative place she'd seen him slide into when things were troubling him.

"Abigail, I have never been more certain of anything in my life than I am about the fact I love you and want you with a desperation that humbles me. Logan and I will hold our expectations for you to the highest standard because we know how much you are capable of. My only explanation for my mistakes tonight is I was frustrated with myself and didn't take time to consider how much better we all would have been served if we'd used a more creative punishment."

"You aren't angry Gage showed up?" Abby noticed her softly spoken question seemed to surprise him. "Even I could see he was mad, and at first, I thought he was mad at me, but then I thought about it and knew someone must have called him. It's going to be like you have two very protective brothers-in-law, you know?"

Both Kalen and Logan both burst out in barking laughter that left Abby staring at them with her mouth gaping open. She knew her wide eyes had to be showing her concern and confusion over their reaction.

"Oh, baby, you have way more protectors than you know. Every man who ever visited the ranch and has met you is going to be calling us out, questioning our motives and intentions." When she gasped, he pulled her on to his lap, so she was facing Kalen. "And that is great because you are right, you are always going to be a handful, and we'll be grateful for all the help we can get in keeping you safe. Now, I'm tired of talking. Let's move this along because I have a burning desire to seal this deal, and that involves Kalen and I both being buried balls deep inside you, little sub."

Despite Logan's crude words, Abby felt herself relax in his arms, and she was pleased to see some of the tension drain from Kalen as well. They were back on more familiar ground, and she was much happier to be interacting in a more *usual* way with them. She knew their relationship was never going to be static, it would be like all other lifetime commitments in that it would have highs and lows.

Kalen took one of her hands in his and pulled it palm up to brush a soft kiss over her delicate skin, then rolled her fingers closed. "Hold that kiss in your heart, love. The most important thing for you to remember always is that we love you. Nothing you say or do will erase that love. And even though there will be times when we don't agree, it won't change the basic truth of our love."

She felt her eyes fill with unshed tears with emotion so strong, she could only nod in response. Logan picked her up, and when he turned her, she saw the other end of the long room bathed in the soft light of what must be a hundred candles. Rose petals covered the bed, and all she could do was stare.

"It's so beautiful. Thank you." Seeing the look of relief and joy cross their faces seemed to erase the last traces of bad energy left lurking in their minds.

Chapter 25

A BBY WOKE UP the next morning and knew without even opening her eyes she was alone in the massive bed. Sighing, she rolled over and looked at the clock and was shocked to see it was nearly noon. There were some habits that were just very difficult to break, and since she'd been rolled out of bed early to complete her chores on the ranch before leaving for school for so many years, sleeping in still made her feel lazy. When she sprang out of bed, she quickly realized her body obviously hadn't been prepared for the shock of being upright, and it took her a few seconds to orient herself.

"Where's the fire, baby?" She spun around to see Logan leaning with his shoulder pressed against the interior of the door frame. He was wearing sinfully low-slung Levis that looked as if they'd been washed a couple hundred times, and with the button open, they were tempting her with promises of what lay below. His bare feet were crossed at the ankles, and every single one of her girly parts responded with a resounding *"Yes"* even though he hadn't actually issued the sexual invitation she saw dancing in his eyes.

"You keep looking at me like that, and you won't be leaving this bedroom for a very long time, baby. Kalen and I have a few things to set up for this evening, but you my sweet sub need to get a move on because Ian has a treat for you, Holly, and Callie." Abby stood blinking at him with what she was sure was a deer in the headlights look. "Still not one of those people who hits the ground running, are you, sweetheart?" She numbly shook her head and was a bit surprised he actually remembered such a small detail about her.

Her brother had often teased her by telling her she would never have survived Special Forces training because she always had woken up dazed and confused for several long minutes. Jace had laughed she'd have been weeded out of BUDS for that alone. She'd regularly pointed out that she was a researcher, not a soldier, and her data didn't seem to care how quickly her mind kicked into gear as long as it was well-drenched in caffeine each morning before being required to perform.

When she blinked again, she realized Kalen had joined Logan, and even though his stance was much more Alpha-Dom than Logan's, his amusement was clear in the way his eyes danced with humor.

"She still isn't a morning person, huh? Amazing when you think about it because her mind works at Mach speed the rest of the time." They both stood looking at her for several seconds, and she could feel her body responding even though her brain wasn't fully online yet. Her nipples were tightening, her pussy flooding with moisture. *Good Lord Almighty they are turning me into a nymphomaniac.*

"Baby, I warned you about that look. Your body is all but shouting its desire, and as much as I'd like to push you right back into that rumpled bed and have my wicked way with you, we need to get you over to Ian and Callie's." Logan stepped forward and took her hand and started leading her to the bathroom. "Get her some coffee, Kalen.

I'll make sure she's started in here. Christ, I hope like hell she doesn't ever have to drive first thing in the morning."

By the time she'd gotten through her shower and a couple of cups of coffee, she was a happy and cognizant camper again. She didn't know where they'd gotten the curve-hugging dress they'd dressed her in, but it was the most beautiful shade of sapphire she'd ever seen. Even though her family had always had plenty of money, neither she nor Jace had been allowed to choose anything but what their parents had considered *reasonable* clothing. Abby was fairly certain a cashmere dress would not have met her mother's standard of reasonable.

Ian met them at the door and studied her closely before nodding as if she'd passed some kind of inspection and turned her toward his housekeeper.

"Inez will show you the way. Now enjoy your treat and try to keep yourself out of mischief. No alcohol, of any kind, for any of you ladies, it that understood?"

Abby smiled and nodded. She understood he didn't want her functioning impaired in any way this evening, and she agreed. She was going to need to keep her wits about her in order to get the confirmation she needed that John Parsons was in some way linked to the Consortium and keep herself and everyone around her safe.

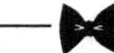

"THERE YOU ARE. Damn, girl, I thought maybe those two hunks of yours might have you tied to the bed. I was just getting ready to mount a covert rescue mission," Callie's voice rang out above the pounding Caribbean beat of Kenny Chesney's *Guitars and Tiki Bars* which was blasting from hidden speakers. Inez had led Abby to the indoor/outdoor pool area behind Ian and Callie's home.

"Holy shit, Batman, look at this place. This wasn't on the tour the last time I was here. What's up with that? Holding out on me?" Abby noticed Holly was sitting in front of a manicurist with her fingers dipped into something that looked like green Jell-O. She made her way over and hugged her new sister.

"Hi, Holly. Please tell me that green shade I see on your face is just a reflection from the goop your fingers are soaking in." Holly looked up at her and started gulping frantically before clasping her hand over her mouth and racing from the room. Abby turned to Callie. "What? What did I say? Fuck a square duck, Jace is going to kick my ass for that."

"Nah, it's not you. She's just pregnant, and that sweet baby doesn't seem to have any respect for his or her mama. Jace told me they've been calling it 'vertical sickness' because anytime she is vertical, she is sick no matter what time of day it is. Oh, fracking fairy farts, I'm supposed to call him if that happens." Just as Callie grabbed her phone, Holly groaned from the next room.

"Don't you dare rat me out, Callie McGregor. I want to play with my friends today. I'm tired of being stuck in that damned bed. What fun is bed if you aren't getting laid?" There was a long pause, then Holly stuck her head out of the door and looked guiltily at Abby, "Oh shit, sorry Abby... that was probably too much information wasn't it?"

For several seconds Abby was too stunned by the fact her first thirty seconds in the room had yielded this much nonsense, but then she couldn't hold it in any longer and burst out laughing. "Damn this is gonna be *fun*." Callie looked at her and grinned.

"Oh yeah, Ian was all about keeping us busy and out from underfoot today so they can plot to overthrow the world without our interference, so he has—" She was interrupted by the chirping of her phone. When she looked down at the screen, her cheeks turned a nice deep shade of red before she answered in a voice so sweet, Abby was worried she might get a cavity just from being nearby. "Hello, sweet husband mine... oh, well... yes, Sir."

Abby watched as Callie's face flushed even more, and her friend started squirming in her chair. She didn't know what Ian was saying to his errant wife, but he was obviously winding her up as tight as an eight-day clock. After a couple of minutes of listening, it was obvious Callie was getting perilously close to orgasm, and Abby could only stand by in dumbfounded silence. When Callie finally whispered "bye" into the phone without coming, Abby suddenly understood what her men had meant by a "variety of ways to punish a wayward sub."

"That was just cruel," was all Abby got out before Callie leaped to her feet and slapped her hand over Abby's mouth and shook her head violently.

Callie leaned close and whispered so quietly, Abby could barely make out the words. "Be careful, this place is wired up so they can hear a fly fart, and I already lost one piece of clothing for tonight, and unless I want to look like a boiled egg with legs, waddling around the club, I'm going to have to be careful. Unless you want everybody to see your ass—ets, you'd better zip it quick, girlfriend."

IAN WATCHED CALLIE on the monitor in his office and shook his head. "Damn, she is the light of my life, but there are times when I wonder what the hell I was thinking." He hit several keys on the screen, and the image of Callie whispering to Abby faded from the screen, and he turned to the men sitting in his office. "There is a part of me that would like nothing more than to fulfill that fantasy for my sweet sub, but there is a much larger part of me that has no intentions of letting the general club membership see her round with our child.

"Having John Parsons in my club tonight is just plain pissing me off. Tell me we have everything in place for this disaster in the making. Convince me our members will be safe as well as the three women out in the pool area who own our hearts." Jace understood his boss's frustration, and there wasn't a man in the room who had more of a vested interest in protecting the women his friend mentioned than he did.

"Well, since you are talking about my wife, my sister, and one of my dearest friends, I'll agree everything we have at our disposal needs to be in place tonight. I've outlined everything in a timeline, and you all have already received copies." He indicated the papers he'd handed each of the men in the room.

"What some of you may not realize is Alex Lamont sent his regrets to Parsons yesterday, and he is sending Mitch Grayson to *fill in*. As I'm sure you can imagine, this is not an accident. We are hoping Mitch can read Parsons. Having inside information would be tremendously helpful, but a man in Parson's position likely knows all about Mitch's abilities by now so it may not be as easy as it could have been."

"Why tell him so far in advance of the change?" Logan's question was expected, and Jace nodded he'd known it was coming.

"Parsons is solid gold obsessive-compulsive. If the change had been sprung too late, he'd have probably canceled, and we would have missed this window of opportunity. Something about this whole mess fucking reeks, and Abby isn't going to be safe until we unravel it. Now, here is the latest development, I haven't even had a chance to brief Ian on this yet." Jace tapped a few keys on the laptop resting in front of him and turned it around for everyone to see.

"For those of you who don't know, this is Sergio Fantella." He heard Kalen and Logan both growl in anger, and he held up his hand to still their protests. "Hear me out. Fantella called me several hours ago and wanted to meet me in a neutral location. I met him at a small coffee shop near Capitol Hill. He took a huge chance meeting with me, but mostly because I know he played my sister, and I wanted to kick his ass for that alone. But I listened to him, and I'm damned glad I did. Quite frankly, I'm not too sure we shouldn't hire him." Laughing at the incredulous looks he got from his team, he handed out another sheet of paper, giving a brief overview of the information the man had provided.

"As you see, he was hired specifically to befriend Abby and lure her to work for the Consortium. The group made it clear he was to 'get the girl by any means necessary,' but it seems Fantella genuinely liked Abby and kept stalling—claiming he needed more time to establish himself in her inner circle, but he admitted he simply wanted to spend more time with her. Anyway, long story short, he is convinced Abby's kidnapping was orchestrated by Parsons, who is evidently working both sides of this and several other *projects* that will be very lucrative for him."

Everyone in the room studied the papers in their hands for long minutes, and when they all seemed to come up for air, it was Ian who spoke.

"You all know what's at stake tonight, and I'd love to keep Callie home under lock and key, but I know any change in routine is going to set off Parsons's alarms. Fuck, I don't know whether to warn her, so she'll be cautious or keep her in the dark, so she doesn't run to the roar."

Jace couldn't contain his laughter because Ian's concern was all too real. Callie was a tiny little thing, but she was a fierce warrior. Hell, she'd gotten in a couple of good jabs on him, and he was a damn Navy SEAL. He smiled to himself because there was no such thing as a *former* SEAL.

"I totally understand your dilemma but can't imagine Abby won't have given her the four eleven on the situation by the time their little spa party is done. I want double trackers on each of them. We've got a couple for Dee and Lizzy as well because I want them working the bar. Holly won't be there because she's battling nausea with everything she has, but it's still kicking her ass. Daphne will be with her in our apartment. She's going to be pissed, but so be it."

Jace ended the meeting after they double checked on the women and found them all enjoying massages. Hearing the grumbling around him when the other men saw what they'd been missing, he shook his head and headed down the hall with Gage to retrieve Holly. He'd seen her race for the bathroom earlier and knew she'd been sick again.

"She didn't call us. Damn it, we told Callie to call one of us if Holly was sick again. I swear she is begging for a couple of swats, and I may call her bluff tonight." Jace's grumbling echoed his own frustration.

Chapter 26

"W HERE'S THE REST of it?" Abby was holding up what looked like a very colorful piece of fabric that would be better used as sheers under drapery than as a dress. When neither Kalen nor Logan responded, she looked from one of them to the other. "No, seriously. Where is the rest of it? You can't seriously expect me to wear a section of somebody's curtains to the club... this isn't going to cover my girly bits, and I really don't want John Parsons seeing my hoo-ha. He's seriously creepy even if he does look like a Greek God."

Both Kalen and Logan's eyes were instantly full of fire. *Oops, that was probably over the top, Abby.* Deciding it was time for damage control, she smiled, then sighed when they both just stood glaring at her.

"Listen, I know my brother is going to be there tonight, and I really don't want to flash him either. I need something that will protect me in case things go to hell. Besides, where are you going to hide the wire?" Logan finally grinned, and she knew she'd been pranked.

"Baby, that is for later. I see your eyes flashing fire but just remember, neither of us said that was what you were wearing to the club tonight—you jumped to that conclusion all on your own."

Kalen's voice didn't hold the same amusement Logan's

had, but he was clearly enjoying her discomfort. "Love, any other night, you would find yourself going to the club stark naked after that little performance. But tonight, you'll be wearing a much more conservative dress for the reasons you already named. Now, your dress is in the closet. The wire is already inside the dress, and we'll test it before we leave the apartment. We normally wouldn't use a separate wire, but we don't really want every fed on the planet knowing all the juicy details of your collar. But remember little sub, each and every word you say will be recorded, so think carefully before you speak. Don't taunt or make any attempt to entrap Parsons. According to intel we received today, it sounds like he has every intention of leaving this island with you in tow."

Logan's large hand wrapped around her upper arm. "That isn't happening, baby. You are not to be out of our sight—is that crystal clear to you? Because I don't want there to be any excuses later. Even if you need to use the ladies room one of us goes with you."

Seriously? They are going to watch me pee? Oh, Cracker Jacks. She heard herself sigh before she nodded her head. *Got it, I need to report all personal needs to the P3.*

"P3? What does that mean?" Logan's voice had gone from teasing to arctic.

Abby jerked her gaze up to his. *Crap, I can't believe I said that out loud.*

"You did indeed say it out loud, baby. And you better explain it quickly. There is no room for error or misunderstanding tonight."

Abby took a deep breath and tried to smile, but knew she'd failed when they both continued to stand with their arms crossed resolutely over their broad shoulders, looking like they'd eaten glass for dinner.

"Piss Police Patrol. That's what my sorority sisters always called it when they wouldn't let me go to the bathroom alone at parties. There was always one girl who didn't drink and always escorted me to the bathroom because I was so much younger than the rest of the sisters. Even though I didn't actually live in the sorority's house until I was eighteen, they never forgot I was one of them, and they tried to include me in most of their crazy adventures when they could. Our campus had a lot of sexual assaults that seemed to happen in or around bathrooms, so it was kind of a safety thing. Sorry, I shouldn't have said anything."

"Abby. Look at me." Logan's voice had lost the ice, but his command was still unmistakable. She hadn't realized she had dropped her eyes to the floor until she found herself looking back up into the smiling faces of both men. "We're thrilled to hear the women you eventually shared a house with took such good care of you. And I hope someday, we can meet some of them to thank them personally."

Abby let out a breath she didn't realize she was holding because she'd worried about their reaction to her story. As usual, Kalen seemed to see right into her soul, and that was as spooky as it was comforting.

"Abigail, don't worry about pleasing or disappointing us with your stories. We want to know everything about you, and listening as you share both good memories and bad will be a large part of that process. I regret how things played out last night because I know in your mind you think it was because your comments were unguarded, so you're reluctant to let your guard down again. But your assessment isn't entirely accurate. It was the timing of the remarks and the attitude that accompanied the words I took issue with. And while my reaction might have been appropriate with a much more experienced and trained submissive, it was disproportionate with you. And love, I can't tell you how much I regret that misjudgment. We both have to work to put that behind us, okay?"

She knew there wasn't any chance of her answering without losing herself to the emotion that was bubbling just below the surface, so she just walked to him and wrapped her arms around his waist and squeezed him. Resting her cheek against his chest and hearing his heartbeat speed up sent satisfaction racing through her soul.

When she finally felt settled enough to speak, she simply said "Thank you. Thank you for loving me and for being strong enough to admit you are human. And thank you for seeing me as someone other than Abby Garrett, the whiz kid whose only value is her research in the international renewable energy and biofuels race."

Chapter 27

KALEN HADN'T EVER considered the possibility anyone would view Abby in such a one-dimensional way. Thinking of her being treated as a commodity whose skills were ripe for the picking made him angrier than he'd been since the night he'd found her in that tiny wood shelter. She'd always been brilliant, and it suddenly appeared as though something he'd always considered a tremendous gift might be as much of a curse as it was a blessing—a possibility he was embarrassed to admit had never occurred to him until this moment.

"Love, you are so very much more than the sum of your parts."

"Well, sweet cheeks, I'll tell you this much—the view from over here is of some mighty *fine* parts." Logan's teasing was evidently just what Abby had needed to break up her melancholy, and Kalen appreciated his friend's insight.

"Well, Sir, my cheeks and I thank you, but I must say, there are other parts of me that are anxious for some of your attention as well."

"Oh, baby, you are playing with fire." Logan's voice was close to a warning growl, but Abby didn't appear to be backing down. She surprised both Kalen and Logan by stepping back out of his arms and running her hands in a torturously slow glide from the tops of her breasts, stopping to pinch her nipples, then slowing sliding her hands over her abdomen and letting her fingers move in slow circles just above her slit.

"Abby, I'm warning you—your body is ours to enjoy, and you're not allowed to play with what is ours unless we specifically tell you to do so."

Kalen pushed his hand between her ass cheeks and through the junction of her thighs and shoved two fingers deep inside her dripping pussy. Her soft gasp was like a magic potion, immediately inflating his cock to near bursting. Leaning down, he scraped his teeth along the top of her shoulder.

"Tell Master Logan what I'm doing to you, love."

"Oh God, your fingers are fucking me."

Kalen loved the breathy way her voice sounded when she was aroused, and he smiled when she had to stop speaking because it was taking all of her concentration to keep the release he felt building inside her from erupting like a volcano.

"Don't tell *me*, Abigail. Tell Master Logan. Try again." He almost laughed at her groan of frustration.

"Master Kalen's fingers are fucking me, and I want to come... oh, I want to come so badly."

Logan tilted his head, and Kalen could see his friend was stalling for time, probably trying to rein in his amusement. In a flash, Kalen knew exactly where Logan was going to go with it, and it took everything he had not to say, "Wait for it...."

Logan finally asked the question that Kalen had known he would, "Why do you want to come badly? That doesn't seem like a very lofty goal for someone with your intelligence or aptitude for efficiency. I think you should be striving for an orgasm that will help you focus on just exactly what you have to do tonight. And I think I can help you with that, baby."

They hadn't planned to take her before they went to the club. After they'd both taken her last night both individually and together before they'd all three collapsed from sheer exhaustion, they'd wanted to give her body a rest until after everything was wrapped up tonight. But just the memory of sliding his throbbing cock in and out of Abby's slick channel had Kalen craving to repeat the experience.

The walls of her vagina had rippled around him with such an intensity last night, he'd been forced to battle back his own release almost from the first moment the broad tip of his penis breached her opening. Feeling her pull him deeper using her pelvic floor muscles had almost caused the top of his head to explode.

Now he watched as Logan bent her over the edge of the bed and drizzled lube over her rear hole, and Kalen's mind was blocking out everything but the urgent need to sink into her heat that seemed to be spinning inside him like a category five tornado. At Logan's nod, Kalen rolled on a condom, stepped behind Abby, and pushed in slowly until she was squirming against him. Giving her bruised ass a swat, he stilled her.

"Be a good girl and hold still so I can take what's mine. Arch your back and present that beautiful ass, love. I'm going to fuck you until Master Logan is in position, then we're going to see if we can't relieve some of that anxiety that is coming off you in waves."

"Please. Please fuck me, I can't take any more teasing. I have to come, or I'm going to die, I just know it." The instant her ass tilted up, Kalen pushed in until his balls were slapping against the engorged lips of her labia.

The feeling of her tight anal muscles clamping down on him was almost painful in its intensity. Logan moved into position and slid to the edge of the bed when Kalen moved Abby's left arm out of his way without ever altering the rhythm of his strokes in and out of her tight little ass.

"Open your eyes and look at me, baby." Logan's voice was gruff, and Kalen knew none of them were going to last long. "Good girl, now suck me. Get me all wet because I'm going to sink into your heat in one hard thrust when the time comes, and you want me as wet as you are when that happens."

Kalen couldn't see Abby's mouth because of the curtain of her hair, but he knew the exact instant she sucked Logan's cock deep because the guttural sound coming from the deepest recesses of his friend's throat was a sure sign of blinding pleasure.

"Fuck me. Your mouth is pure sin with sweet lips, baby. Oh, Christ, that's enough."

Kalen bent his knees against the backs of Abby's thighs and used that leverage to help him lift her knees and move forward. He pulled out partway and waited for Logan's quick nod, indicating his cock was lined up with Abby's pussy. When Kalen saw the nod, he lowered Abby down just as Logan thrust up hard and fast, and true to his word, he was as deep as he could go in a split second. Abby's scream was pure raw desire set to the lyrical sound of her voice. He and Logan took their cue from her and began alternating their thrusts until Kalen was starting to see stars.

His mind registered an awareness the orgasm rolling over him was going to be explosive, but nothing prepared him for the burst of white light that exploded behind his eyelids when Abby's entire body stiffened and locked down on his cock hard enough that his own release was literally ripped from his body in an almost violent storm. At the same time Abby screamed their names, they both shouted hers. Kalen was glad she fell onto Logan because, at that moment, he wasn't sure he'd have been able to catch her. Hell, he was barely able to remain standing himself.

When he finally realized the colors and dots that had marked his vision had faded, he managed to pull his cock from her ass and quickly went to the bathroom to clean up. Returning in just a few seconds, he found Abby still impaled on Logan's cock, and her dark eyes were still dazed. It took them several minutes to clean themselves up and get dressed. Kalen noted smugly Abby was still a little wobbly as they made their way down the hall to the club. He turned to Abby and kissed her in a way he knew would convey his support.

"Let's do this. We believe in you, love, let's go—it's show time." As he opened the door, he heard Logan telling her how beautiful she looked and how great he knew tonight was going to go. *You have to love a man with older sisters.*

Logan had known exactly what to say to send Abby into the room, looking like she owned it. With just that small bit of praise to boost to her self-confidence, Abby had taken on a luminescence, and its effect on those around her was almost magnetic. People were drawn to her even more than usual, and from across the room, Kalen saw John Parsons's eyes lock onto her like a heat-seeking missile.

Chapter 28

THERE WAS NO mistaking the sated, almost dreamy expression on Abby Garrett's face as she walked into the club from what must have been a private entrance. Even though there were several people surrounding him, including Mitch Grayson, who had evidently been assigned the task of babysitting him, John didn't see anyone but Abby after she walked into the room. Christ, she was even more gorgeous than he remembered.

He'd met her once when she'd talked to him about her safety concerns related to the Consortium, but she'd been covered head to toe in some God-awful tweed pantsuit that hid the gorgeous body he saw now. The sparkling red dress she was wearing tonight might be more conservative than most of the submissives were wearing, but it was still leaving little to the imagination. The top was cut so low, he wondered if the tops of her areolas were visible up close. Suddenly, he understood why Fantella had been so anxious to spend more time with the woman. She might be some over-the-top genius who'd made a trillion-dollar discovery, but she was also fucking hot. Suddenly, this mission had just become a whole lot more interesting.

"INCOMING AT ELEVEN o'clock and three o'clock." Kalen's words came quietly over his earbud, but Logan hadn't missed them. He'd seen Parsons at the eleven o'clock position when they'd walked in, so no need to look there. But he slowly rotated enough to see Callie making her way toward them, and if he wasn't mistaken, Ian's sweet wife was purposely timing her arrival to coincide with Parsons's approach.

"I swear, I'm gonna paddle her sweet ass myself if Ian doesn't do it. Abby, send her after something, get her away from you if you can." Logan was speaking against her ear and running his hands over her shoulders so to an outsider, it would look like nothing more than an intimate conversation between lovers.

John Parsons stopped in front of Abby, his eyes raking down her in a move so blatantly that of a sexual predator, Logan nearly came unhinged. The only thing that kept him from stepping in front of her was feeling the subtle shift of her body away from Parsons and toward Callie.

In a flash of insight, Logan realized Callie's move had been calculated with a strategic precision that would make a general proud. She'd given Abby a way to shift her focus that would never be construed as anything other than friends greeting each other. Callie's sweet voice rang loud enough everyone within earshot would have noted her enthusiasm.

"Ohhh, I'm so excited to see you. It's been forever, and girlfriend, we really need to talk about that gorgeous choker."

Callie's high-pitched squeal of delight drew even more attention, and Logan bit back a smile at the look on Parson's face. Clearly, the man hadn't done his homework because he was looking at the woman who held Ian McGregor's heart in her tiny hand like she was a virulent gnat. Logan's pride in her soared when Abby looked to him for approval before moving out of his hold to embrace her friend. She had not only done so with the natural ease of a well-trained sub, but she had also sent a clear message to Parsons in the process.

Jace and Ian had pointed out it would be very difficult for an untrained sub to track and obey two Masters, and if she had two men flanking her, it might be more than Parsons would want to face, so Kalen was working with the security team, and Logan was her escort for the evening. Logan and Kalen knew having one-on-one time with Abby was going to be crucial to the long-term success of the relationship they envisioned them sharing for the rest of their lives. Even though Kalen was taking a back seat this evening, he had refused to be anywhere he wouldn't be "eyes-on" with Abby. Even though Logan couldn't see his friend at this particular moment, he didn't doubt for a minute he was close by.

"Hi, Callie, I'm glad to see you too." Abby ran her fingers over her collar and smiled. "It's beautiful, isn't it? It was a gift, and I'm looking forward to sharing all the juicy details with you." Evidently, John Parsons was tired of being ignored because he cleared his throat to get Abby's attention.

ABBY TURNED TO face John Parsons and almost cringed at the look he was giving her. She was sure if there was ever such a thing as "visual sexual assault," she'd just become a victim.

"Mr. Parsons? I didn't realize you were a member of Club Isola. How are you?" Abby intended to play this off as a casual meeting and keep the fact she'd known she would be seeing him off the table. She'd played enough poker with her dads and brother to know better than to tip her hand too soon.

"Abby Garrett, imagine seeing you here. And I must say, you look lovely. Oh, yes indeed—very lovely." The weasel glanced at Callie, and his feral grin went hot as he raked his gaze to Callie's low-cut dress that was prominently displaying her ample cleavage. Abby had laughed so hard earlier that day at her new friend's delight in the fact she actually had "breasts" now that she was pregnant. Callie had told her she'd told her gynecologist he'd better figure out a way for her to "keep the boobs" after the baby was born because she wasn't giving them up.

"Abby, please introduce me to your lovely friend." *Not in a gazillion years, you asshat.*

Callie took a step forward no one would interpret as friendly, and Abby saw, for the first time, why Ian called her *Carlin.* Callie stuck her hand out, and in a voice that might have sounded like pure sugar, but was filled with loathing, said, "There is no reason to put my friend in such an awkward position when I am so clearly capable of *re*-introducing myself. I'm Callie McGregor, and we've already met in my husband's office. How do you know Abby?"

Abby was literally biting the insides of her mouth to keep from smiling. Oh, yeah, "little champion" was a very accurate description of Callie McGregor. To his credit, Parsons seemed to recover quickly.

"Oh, yes, I'm sorry, I'd forgotten our earlier encounter." *Liar.* "Abby and I have a mutual interest in renewable energy."

He'd taken Callie's outstretched hand and rather than shake it he pulled it towards his lips, fully intending to kiss it, but Callie had other ideas and pulled her hand from his grasp.

"Mr. Parsons, that would be inappropriate. I thought my husband made the situation perfectly clear when he referred to me as his wife. I'm Mrs. Callie McGregor, Ian McGregor is my husband and my Master. I can assure you, that he would not approve of that action."

At that moment, Ian stepped up behind Callie and wrapped his arm protectively around her, letting his left hand caress his wife's baby bump. Abby saw fire in his eyes before they softened when he leaned down and softly bit Callie's bare shoulder.

"*Carlin*, you are absolutely right. You please me very much, my love." When Ian returned his gaze to Parsons, the warmth was gone, and the businessman Abby had only seen on rare occasions was in place.

"Mr. Parsons, if you have any questions about my club, please don't hesitate to let me know. I'll ask that you stay close to your sponsor this evening. It is my understanding Alex Lamont had to bow out and sent Mitch Grayson in his stead, is that correct?" Mitch stepped up and shook hands with Ian.

"Hi, Ian." Then, turning he smiled at Callie. "Callie, you look wonderful, and that baby is mighty lucky to have such a sweet mama. Rissa sends her love and has volunteered to come and stay for a few days with you, assuming she can wrangle Bryant and me into taking over care of 'Betsy the Destroyer.' Don't laugh, I'm not kidding. She may look like her mama, but I'm convinced she is a reincarnated terrorist." Everyone laughed, and Abby saw Mitch slap Parsons on the back. "Hey, I didn't ask you if you have a wife or children."

Mitch had managed to touch Parsons twice since he'd joined them, and Abby had heard the men say he'd have a better chance of *reading* the man if he could touch him. Since Mitch had convinced her of the validity of his "gift" as he called it, she'd been fascinated to learn everything she could about how it worked. Parsons answered Mitch's question but kept his eyes glued on her, and his look made Abby more nervous than she could ever remember being.

"No, no wife or children... yet. But I must admit, the idea is sounding better and better as I get older." Abby couldn't hold back the shudder that ran up her spine. Parsons hadn't missed it, and neither had Logan.

"Cold, baby? There does seem to be a bit of a draft right here. Let's move on. Why don't you and Callie have a seat over there while Ian and I get you something to drink?" He'd motioned to the sitting area that was the most open, and Abby knew it had been chosen in advance for its visibility. Sitting on the small seat next to Callie, Abby smiled at her friend.

"Damn, girlfriend, you are something. Are you sure you aren't a Texas girl?" Callie's laugh was cut short when she placed her hand over her tummy and frowned. "Hey, what's that frown for? Is something wrong? Do you need me to get Ian?"

"Shhh. Geez, Abby. You've probably just alerted security in three states. Damn. It was just a little muscle spasm. I've been having them all day in my back, so I'm sure this is just my front wanting equal time."

Abby wasn't convinced, and when she looked toward the bar, she saw Ian holding his phone and frowning in their direction. "Uh oh, I'm sorry," was all she managed to get out before Callie looked up and saw Ian.

"Well, crap on a cracker. Shoot, I never get to have any fun. But I'm going to look on the bright side, the Wildcats are playing tonight, so I'll have to settle for watching them whoop up on your Longhorns."

"Dream on, sister. Not this day... probably not any day." Abby laughed at their easy rivalry. When she'd learned Callie had spent time at her aunt and uncle's in Kansas, they'd started talking about sports teams and quickly discovered a mutual interest in football.

"*Carlin*, talk to me love." Ian had knelt in front of Callie and held both of her small hands in one of his much larger ones while he tunneled the fingers of his other hand under Callie's hair to grasp her nape. Before she became involved in a D/s relationship, the significance of the move might have escaped Abby's attention. But now, the way Ian's hand manacled Callie's wrists while his other hand gripped her neck with a gentle force that centered her attention on him was such a blatant display of Dominance, it sent tingles racing up Abby's spine.

"I'm sure it's just muscles spasms, Master. My body just keeps... well, stretching, and sometimes, I don't think it's got anymore stretch to give." Callie suddenly looked like she was trying very hard to not cry, and Abby wondered just how painful her "spasms" were and how often they were occurring. But then Callie took a deep breath and let it out slowly.

"I'm sorry. I don't want to disrupt your plans, but maybe you could have someone from the staff drive me home?" Abby could see the perspiration suddenly beading on Callie's forehead, and her breathing was shallow as well. Ian leaned forward and kissed Callie's damp forehead.

"No, my love, no one from the staff is going to drive you home." Abby noticed Callie's shoulders droop just a fraction and knew her friend was disappointed but obviously wasn't planning to object. Just as Abby started to speak, she felt a soft squeeze on her shoulder that stopped her. Ian turned to Jace who seemed to have materialized out of thin air in front of them and said, "I'm taking Callie home. Activate B-Plan, and I'll keep you posted."

Abby didn't know for sure, but if she was a betting woman, she'd go with "B-Plan" being code for their plan of action for when Callie went into labor. And knowing her brother and Ian, the entire thing was probably mapped out with military precision. Mitch sat down next to Callie, and Abby saw her friend smile at him.

"Sweetness, you are rushing things a bit, no? But sometimes babies have their own timelines, and this one is just really anxious to say hello. You are going to be an amazing mother." Abby laughed out loud when Mitch started to stand up, then quickly sat back down and touched Callie on the end of her nose with his finger. "And be a good little sub and don't call Rissa before I get the scoop, or I'll never hear the end of it."

Ian scooped Callie up into his arms and began making his way slowly toward the closest exit. Abby watched as people seemed to scatter in several directions when Ian started giving orders with quiet authority without ever letting his attention move from his wife. He was obviously accustomed to having his instructions followed because he didn't bother to check that his directives were heeded, he simply continued out the door.

Abby hadn't even realized she was alone until the hair on the back of her neck stood up on end, and she heard John Parsons's grating voice.

"Well, seems I'm going to get a chance to speak with you without your guard dogs growling at me after all. Come along, Abby."

Chapter 29

L OGAN STEPPED BACK into the small sitting area and stared at the empty sofa. *What the fuck?* Where was Abby? And where the hell was Kalen? It wasn't like him to go off-grid when they both knew how imperative it was to keep a close watch on Abby. Why in the hell had she moved? Sure, he hadn't specifically told her to stay put, but they had made it clear she wasn't supposed to go anywhere without one of the security team. Callie going into labor had thrown everyone a curve because she wasn't due for another two weeks, but he hadn't been gone more than a couple of minutes.

He pulled his phone from his pocket just as it rang. "Where is she?" Logan's internal alarms were going off like clanging gongs in his head, and he hoped he would be able to hear whoever was on the other end over the din. Tony Dent's voice was clipped and efficient.

"We've got her. She's westbound on a cart. Parsons is making her drive, and she is pretending she doesn't know her way around the island, so she is driving like a geriatric turtle. Hell, I can hop one-legged faster. She's a kick, man." Logan wanted to bat the youngest member of their team upside the head but just waited because he could hear the clicking of keys.

"Okay, Mitch Grayson just joined me in the control

room, so this is going to get a lot more interesting. He's taking the com."

"Grayson here. Our girl is keeping Parsons talking and getting lots of good stuff, so I'd say he isn't planning on letting her go. Looks like your guys have already snatched up his escape boat driver, and he's singing like a canary. She's been recording since he walked her out the back door, and as slow as she's driving, I'll be surprised if they get to the boat before sunrise so we may have to figure out a different way to hide your team."

Logan could hear the amusement in Mitch's voice, and that gave him hope he was going to have Abby safely back in his arms soon. He was already sprinting down the path she had taken.

When he'd heard Mitch call for all units to report their locations, there had been a voice he didn't recognize, and from the location he'd given, he was the one who was going to engage Parsons and Abby first. Even though the island wasn't large, it was covered in trees and lushly landscaped gardens with intricately winding trails that offered a plethora of hiding places, so he was grateful the man said he was right behind the cart.

ABBY WASN'T SURE how much longer she was going to be able to stall because Parsons was getting pissed about her driving so slow. It was true, she was driving slow enough, she was worried the shadow she'd caught in the small rearview mirror was going to overtake them. Hell, if it was a member of Jace's security detail, the guy was probably having trouble walking slow enough to not walk right up their asses.

"So, John, what's the plan? What makes you think I'm going to help you or whoever is signing your paycheck this week?" She wasn't even trying to keep the disdain from her voice because she didn't know for sure he was working outside his authority as a United States government employee, but the fact he worked for the C.I.A. and they were still on U.S. soil was pretty telling.

"You know what, Abby? We could have been a hell of a team, but you were just too fucking dim to figure it out. Honestly, I'm starting to doubt you're really as smart as everybody swears you are. The Consortium has offered you obscene amounts of money to work for them, and you have refused every generous offer. The one guy we send to bring you in that you'll even give the time of day, you win over, and he refuses to use any of our *suggestions*."

"You're an ass. Has anybody ever told you that? My dad described a guy like you once… said it was like someone had taken a box of shit and wrapped it up in a real pretty package." Abby saw the back of his hand in her peripheral vision a split second before it connected with her right cheek.

Two things went through her mind at the exact same time—first was the man had just signed his own death warrant because she was sure Logan or Kalen would kill him, and if he somehow managed to worm past them, Jace and Gage would be waiting. The second thought was she'd just been given the perfect opportunity to escape, so she yelped and rolled smoothly out of the cart, hitting the ground running.

She'd rolled to her feet and taken off a lot smoother this time than she had when she'd rolled out of the trunk. *Fuck it, one more kidnapping, and I'm gonna be a pro.* She'd only taken a few steps when she was grabbed and spun around just as she heard a gunshot and felt a sting in her shoulder. She fell backward, and the man who had spun her around landed on top of her, knocking the wind out of her.

Abby was gasping for air under the man's weight, and her mind flashed to the time she'd fallen out of the tree in her parents' yard and landed on her back. Jace had been the first one to her. He'd tried to calm her down when he'd seen the panic in her eyes, but she'd been convinced she was dying. Later, she'd read everything she could get her hands on about the phenomenon, and she still hated the feeling. Trying desperately to get oxygen into her lungs, she was relieved when she was finally able to roll out from under the man who had just saved her. But her relief was short-lived when she realized it was Sergio Fantella's weight she'd just escaped.

As she was trying to get her feet under her again, she felt a hand clamp over her upper arms and yank her to her feet. Abby heard her own yelp of pain at the motion in her shoulder, but her mind was so clouded by fear, she barely registered her response before she kicked back with all her strength and connected with her assailant's shin. When the hard hands didn't release her, something in her mind simply snapped, and she went into warrior princess mode.

KALEN HADN'T BEEN far behind Fantella and had been closing in fast when he'd seen Abby appear out of the darkness. As she'd approached Fantella, the man had wrapped his arms around her and swung them both around just as Kalen had seen the flash and heard the gun's report. Kalen rolled the man off Abby because he could hear her gasping for air, and he'd been worried the shot had passed through the man who had saved her and caught her as well. Kalen had just managed to free her when she'd started trying to scramble to her feet to run again—damn, he was proud of her—until he'd picked her up and heard her gasp in pain a split second before she went completely wild against him.

She'd kicked him with enough force, she might well have broken his tibia if he hadn't had on his leathers and high-topped boots. After she sunk her elbow into his solar plexus, he'd barely been able to get out a snarled, "Abigail. Stop." It had taken just a second for her mind to process his words before she'd gone completely limp in his arms. He set her on her feet, and when he turned her, so she was facing him, he felt the unmistakable stickiness of blood on his fingers. "You're hurt. Where?"

Kalen had no sooner spoken the words than the entire island seemed to light up. There were carts and spotlights everywhere and a helicopter overhead with a large spotlight they were keeping trained on the CIA's Deputy Director. Parsons was currently lying face down on the gravel path with Jace Garrett's boot in the center of his back while a small man in a dark suit that all but shouted FBI agent read him his rights.

There were several people kneeling around Fantella, and Kalen could see they were trying to stop the blood that was still running a steady stream from the gaping wound in the man's back. Fantella had taken the bullet intended for Abby when he'd spun her around to shield her body with his own. If the man lived, Kalen knew he and Logan were going to do what they could to help him because it was likely he'd just put himself very high on the Consortium's hit list.

"Something stung my shoulder, but it's alright. Is he dead?" Kalen felt her entire body shudder at the possibility. She kept her face buried in his chest, and he was grateful she wasn't watching the pandemonium playing out around them, but he needed to check out her "sting" because he had a sinking feeling it was more than that. Pulling back just a bit so he could look down into her eyes, he gave her what he hoped was a huge smile.

"Love, you are amazing. Not only did you escape another kidnapping, you nearly dropped me with a couple of those blows. I'm very proud of you, and I know Logan will be as well. Hell, there's going to be no living with your brother now." Kalen watched as Logan stepped up behind her, and his expression went from concern to panic.

"What the fuck? Come on, baby, we need to get you back up to the club right now." That was when Kalen looked down at his own shirt and was shocked by how much blood he saw. Logan picked her up, and they quickly commandeered one of the many carts and headed back to the club just as Ian's personal helicopter was taking off, and a medevac unit was landing.

Don Whiteside was already busy working on Fantella, but Kalen knew there were several other medical professionals who were club members, so they headed right to the small infirmary inside the club. Lisa Crain didn't hesitate to help them assess Abby's injury despite the fact she was actually a pediatrician.

Kalen had never talked to Lisa outside of Club Isola and was dumbfounded as he watched her change from submissive to physician in the blink of an eye. She was a study in contrasts that was for sure. Her husband and

Master was leaning back against the wall with his arms crossed over his massive chest, smiling.

"Amazing, isn't she?" Kalen could only nod numbly. *Fucking incredible would be closer.* "The first time I saw her at work, she was working triage in the emergency room at Children's Hospital downtown. I'm sure I had the same look on my face you have now.

Kalen knew Mark Crain was a detective for the DC police because Jace had been trying to recruit the man for almost a year. Lisa had stopped the bleeding and given Abby something for the pain, but she'd also said Abby was going to need surgery to remove the bullet since there was no exit wound. When Kalen's phone vibrated in his pocket, Tony Dent informed him he'd heard the good doctor's words and had already summoned another helicopter. Kalen thanked him, moved over to Abby, discreetly deactivated the audio on her collar, and made a mental note to talk to Mitch about the need for a way to do it remotely.

Logan was pushing the hair back from Abby's forehead, and Kalen smiled at the image of his friend's overtly affectionate gesture. Both he and Logan were known as fairly strict Doms who prided themselves on having helped several Doms tame their unruly subs, but there was something about Abby's core of vulnerability that pulled the nurturer in both him and Logan to the surface.

Abby's voice was airy and her words slightly slurred from the pain medication Lisa had given her, but he still heard the worry in her questions about Sergio Fantella. Logan was assuring her he was in the best possible hands, and Don Whiteside had accompanied him to the hospital.

"Oh Lord, you sent him with Dr. Donnie Dark? That wasn't nice of you all... nope, not nice at all. Boy, you are up to your asses in alligators now. Holly is gonna kick your cute booties, you just watch and..." Kalen wanted to laugh out loud when she fell asleep in the middle of a sentence, but he was too worried about her despite Lisa's assurance the wound wasn't life-threatening.

Logan looked up and frowned. "I know it shouldn't bother me she is worried about him, but it does. But from what you've told me, he saved her life, so we're always going to owe the bastard for that."

Kalen smiled because he could see Logan struggling with the karma of holding on to anger that was actually nothing but jealousy. His friends might tease him about his philosophy studies, but they often struggled with the same age-old questions without ever realizing it.

Chapter 30

A BBY WOKE UP suddenly when she heard Logan's voice telling her to stop struggling. *Struggling?* Damn, her mouth felt like it had been stuffed with cotton balls, and her shoulder felt like it was on fire. She tried to open her eyes, but the lids felt like they each weighed a ton. She mentally reviewed what she remembered and her concern for Sergio. Just as she was getting ready to ask about the man she had once considered a close friend, she felt another presence on her other side. When she finally managed to open her eyes, she saw both Logan and Kalen watching her.

"Love, I want you to know Sergio Fantella is out of surgery and seems to be doing well. During his transport to the hospital, he regained consciousness enough to ask that someone contact his partner." Kalen's voice might have sounded sweet and loving, but it was almost like there was a strange vibration coming off him.

"She needs a drink of water and some pain meds. I'll get the nurse." Abby was grateful Logan had figured out how much she was struggling, but on the other hand, she was a real lightweight with pain meds. She would probably chatter like a magpie, and God only knew what she was likely to say.

The ice chips they gave her helped her parched throat,

but the nurse who had injected the pain medication into her IV was more interested in flirting with Logan and Kalen than she was in caring for her. Abby wished the slut had been on her other side, the one that wasn't bandaged and wrapped up so tight she felt like a half-mummy. After the wannabe poacher left the room, Logan burst out laughing.

"Baby, I could hear most of that, and even if I hadn't been able to hear your thoughts, your facial expressions would have given you away." Abby smiled at him and tried to shrug. Just that tiny movement sent a bolt of white-hot pain through her shoulder.

"Fuck me. I wish they'd left the bullet in, my shoulder didn't hurt this much before they *fixed* it." She knew she sounded like a whiny child, but she had never been a good patient.

Abby heard the door open, and Holly stepped into her view. "Oh, Abby, I was so worried about you. Damn, I can't leave you or Callie alone for a minute. You two are grounded."

Laughing at her sister-in-law, Abby asked, "Practicing up on your parenting skills, Holly?"

"Yep. I figure any child who has you for an aunt is going to be a real handful, so I want to get a head start." Holly might be a little bit of a thing, but she bulldozed past Kalen to take Abby's hand. "Oh, you should see Callie... well more like you should hear Callie. Holy frankincense, who knew that many bad words could come out of such a tiny woman. Yikes. Good Lord, she's downright creative sometimes. I took notes." The look of self-satisfaction on Holly's sweet face struck Abby as funny for some reason, and she started giggling. The puzzled look on Holly's face only added to her hysterical laughter until tears were streaming down both her cheeks.

"They gave her pain meds, didn't they?" Jace's voice rang out from the end of the bed.

"Oh, looky… my big brother is here. Did you bring me a root beer? You always smuggled in root beer when I was sick. Where is it? I'm really thirsty, and I wondered about that boyfriend thing Kalen mentioned. I'm betting Kalen's all pissy because I didn't mention that part. But I wanted Kalen and Logan to trust me because they should, not because the guy I thought was hot wasn't really hot for me." The room was starting to spin, and she felt hot all of a sudden, but she managed to turn to Holly and ask, "That made sense, right?"

"Yep, it was all perfectly clear. I understood every single word. Now, time for you to sleep, sweet sister." Abby felt Holly's cool fingers brushing over the eyes, and the comforting touch was all it took for the darkness to claim her.

LOGAN WATCHED THE whole thing but was speechless. When he looked up at Jace and blinked, Abby's brother just shook his head. "Happens every time. She has the lowest tolerance for medications of anyone I've ever known. I'm glad I sent word ahead to the hospital warning them. I also talked to everyone I could about her penicillin allergy. Damn, I can't believe she remembered the root beer. I did always smuggle it into her when she was sick because Mom always wanted her to drink Sprite, and she hated it with a passion. I'd drink her Sprite, and she'd guzzle the root beer before Mom came to check on her."

Logan started to laugh, then stopped himself when he thought about her words. She was absolutely right. They should have trusted her just as they'd asked her to trust them. It was a mistake he regretted and didn't plan to repeat. He was also sure she would have found it humiliating to discover the man she'd been pining after had been paid to befriend her. *Damn, talk about your double whammy.*

Jace stepped up to Holly and smiled down at her indulgently. "Why did you tell her she was making sense?"

"I didn't say she was making sense. I said I understood every word she said… and I did, every single word she said was English, and I didn't have any trouble understanding any of them. Now… the order and meaning was a complete mystery, but the words themselves were a cinch."

Logan chuckled because only a writer would be able to twist words around like that until the argument sounded perfectly reasonable. He pitied Jace and Gage because their woman was going to keep them on their toes for sure.

"I'll sit with her for a bit if you guys want to go to the waiting room for your strategy-thingy."

Logan realized he, Kalen, Jace, and Gage had all four turned to her at the same moment and spoken in perfect unison, "Strategy *thingy*?" Evidently, she'd found the looks on their faces amusing because Holly started laughing and was still snickering as they all stalked into the hall. But, by the time they settled in the small waiting room, they were all shaking their heads and laughing too. Jace gave them a quick update, and Logan could see the man was furious his sister had been hurt but proud as hell of the way she'd handled herself.

"The information she managed to get from Parsons is going to go a long way toward his conviction. At this point, it doesn't look like the Consortium knew Parsons had authorized Abby's abduction. That's not to say they wouldn't have approved, but they were offering a five-million-dollar bonus to whoever brought her on board, so I'm surprised she hasn't had more trouble than she has. They have now withdrawn that offer, so she should be safe—at least for the time being, anyway." When Kalen and Logan explained Abby's comments about Sergio Fantella, Jace didn't say anything for several long seconds.

"She's right. I think we often demand our subs' obedience and expect them to respond appropriately to our Dominance, but we don't always respect them beyond those parameters. Ian has Daphne managing Fantella's care, so I'll let her know to include his partner in all the decisions."

Gage hadn't said much while they'd been talking, but as they all stood, he looked at both Logan and Kalen and said, "Abby has *two* brothers who love her, and Ian isn't far behind. Take very good care of her and don't ever forget how lucky you are to have this opportunity with her."

Logan nodded, and Kalen simply said, "Agreed."

IAN HELD CALLIE'S hand and reassured her even as he questioned whether or not he was lying to her. He'd managed to get out of the room for a couple of minutes almost an hour earlier, and the doctor had informed him their baby would be delivered within the next half hour, and now it had been twice that long and Callie was exhausted. The man was supposed to be the best obstetrician in the city, and he couldn't predict a delivery any closer than this?

One thing Ian had learned was his wife had fingers that could give a pair of Vise-Grips a run for its money. Each contraction had brought a lockdown of her tiny fingers on his, and they'd nearly gone numb before she'd released them the last time. At first, he'd been mortified by her cursing, but one of the nurses had assured him she'd heard much worse, and it was perfectly normal. Suddenly, Callie looked up at him with sad eyes.

"I can't do this anymore, Master. I've changed my mind, I don't want a baby, let's just go home? Can you please just take me home?" The fact she'd called him Master in front of people outside of their lifestyle told him exactly how exhausted and desperate she was.

"*Carlin*, you don't mean that. You've been so brave, and I'm so proud of you. Don't give up now. I'm very anxious to meet our child."

The doctor walked in, and his booming voice was the perfect distraction. "I agree with your husband, Callie. Let's get this show on the road and deliver this baby, what do you say?" Callie's look was stunned disbelief, and her voice was almost arctic.

"You mean I just had to wait for you to decide to do it? That's it? I've been stuck in this bed for hours, being squeezed from the inside out like a fucking orange, and you waltz in here, all chipper, happy as a clam, and suddenly, it's showtime?"

Ian was completely speechless by Callie's behavior. He'd never heard her talk to anyone so disrespectfully, but when he looked at the elderly doctor, the man actually looked amused.

"Yep, that's how it works alright. We don't put that in any of the brochures because women would have stopped having babies a long time ago and think about how that would have worked out." Ian had to give the man credit, he was thick-skinned and obviously had a great sense of humor. But if what the nurse had said about the acting out being normal, he probably needed to be very resilient.

From the time the doctor walked in until Ian was cutting the cord and holding his child had only been minutes, but they had been so profoundly moving, Ian worried he'd drop his beautiful daughter. Carly McGregor had her mother's petite frame and nose, but her dark hair, eyes, and skin tone were all her daddy, and he couldn't be any prouder. By the time the staff finished poking and prodding both mother and child and settled them in their private suite, both of his girls were fast asleep.

Quietly exiting the room, he wasn't at all surprised to see Daphne standing just outside the door. The damn woman was part spook if you asked Ian. Her sixth sense was incredible.

"Congratulations, Ian. I can't begin to tell you how happy I am for you." The sincerity in her eyes touched him, and he pulled her into a hug so suddenly, he heard her sharp intake of breath in surprise.

"I can't think of anyone else I'd rather share this moment with. Thank you for your constant love and support. Even though I don't tell you nearly often enough as I should how important you are to me, we both know I couldn't have done any of this without you."

"I'm not sure that is true... but thank you. Now, before you make me all mushy, I have some updates for you." Ian listened as Daphne brought him up to speed on everything that had been happening while Callie had been struggling to bring Carly into the world. She ended by telling him she was already fielding calls from all over the world about the choker Abby had been wearing, and just that quickly, the tiny bundle of joy in the next room launched her own high-tech jewelry line.

Chapter 31

Four weeks later

C ALLIE SAT IN the rocker, nursing Carly and watching Abby pace back and forth like a caged animal. "I really don't understand why you are so wound up? I told you how to solve this problem two weeks ago, but you weren't interested in my battery-operated solution as I recall." Callie had tried to keep the amusement out of her voice, but she knew she'd failed miserably. Okay, maybe she hadn't really tried all that hard, but she'd actually considered it, so that should count for something.

Looking up, she noticed Abby had stopped right in front of her and was looking at Carly as if her "niece" had hung the moon and the stars.

"She is so beautiful, and she is going to be brilliant too... we're going to see to it. But I want her to have lots of cousins, and how is she going to have that if I can't get laid? Holly can't be expected to do it all alone. Damn it to hell, this stinks. Besides... it's like someone gave me this great toy and let me play with it just long enough to get totally hooked, then they take it back."

At that moment Holly came into the room and immediately put her hands over her ears before making herself comfortable on the sofa and kicking off her shoes. When she put her small, but swollen feet on the table in front of her, she smiled at Abby.

"You still whining about not getting any? Didn't we already beat this horse to death? You want to talk about something important? Look at those balloons at the ends of my legs. This is starting to make me rethink that whole 'barefoot and pregnant' saying. I'm betting it was started by some woman who couldn't get her damned shoes on. Hell, she was only barefoot by necessity, not because of some man's overly inflated sense of power and control." She cringed when Carly stirred at the sharpness in her voice. Callie's soft giggle and soothing words to the baby made her friends grin.

"It's okay, sweet baby. Aunt Holly and Aunt Abby just have their panties in a twist. But it's all good because I think they have forgotten how daddy has this room wired, so it's almost like it is full of people. People who like to record things and share them with their friends."

"Cra... yfish. It's like living in some da... ng James Bond movie." When Callie started giggling again, Abby merely shrugged. "Hey, I'm getting better. Kat's been coaching me on substitute words. She's the queen of all things crazy, I tell you. I can hardly wait to go visit her next week. I was supposed to meet with Alex and Zach in Denver so their dad could sit in, but we changed it to ShadowDance. It's easier for them to secure, and this way, I get to spend some time with Katarina as well. She's also going to help me make my presentation for Garrett Oil's Board of Directors a multi-media spectacular... her words, not mine, by the way.

"I'm going to be asking them for a huge chunk of change, and I want them completely on board. The Lamonts are already committed, and of course, McGregor

Holdings has always seen the potential. Ironic the company my parents still own the majority of stock in is my biggest worry."

"Why do you have to sell it to them if your family owns the majority voting shares?"

Holly answered Callie's question before Abby had a chance, explaining in far clearer terms than Abby might have used. Holly outlined how having the board solidly behind the project was important to the continued strength of the company that had only gone public just a few years earlier.

"Okay, enough business. Let's get back to this no sex issue. I got my stitches out early this morning, and I got the green light from the plastic surgeon for all things kinky. So, I stopped by a couple of specialty shops on the way back from the doctor's office. I didn't tell anyone I went because I wanted to surprise them... what?" Abby was looking back and forth between Callie and Holly, who had both dissolved into fits of giggles.

Callie shook her head and finally regained enough composure to speak. "Good God, Gertie. You ought to get kicked out of Mensa for that one. I mean really? You can't see how insanely dim that statement was? *Hello*... you are wearing a choker that has a kick ass... ets and take names tracking device. I'll bet you dollars to donuts that your car has at least one tracker, too."

Abby just stared at her aghast. "Are you kidding me? They'd track my car?"

"A nursing mother never kids about donuts... *not ever*. And what about the choker? You didn't mention that one." There was something in Abby's expression that set off Callie's alarms. "What did you do? Oh, girlfriend, you are in huge trouble. I can feel it. Holy hel... icopters. I should make you leave right now, so my baby doesn't get caught in the lightning storm I feel brewing all around you. Oh mercy, I can't believe you found a way to tamper with it already? I mean, I'm sure they knew you would at some point, but it's been less than a month, for heaven's sake."

The words had barely left her mouth when the door of the nursery opened, and the room filled with men. Callie rolled her eyes and silently mouthed "sorry" to Abby. Callie grimaced as she took in their expressions. A standoff between the Hatfields and the McCoys would have looked more amiable.

Jace and Gage flanked Holly and looked her over from head to toe as if deciding whether she was physically capable of walking out of the room. Callie thought Ian was overly protective while she'd been pregnant with Carly, but she was suddenly glad she'd only had one alpha male to contend with during those months.

Callie looked up to see Ian studying her carefully. When he winked at her, she bit back a grin. Just that small gesture let her know she was in for a show, and she'd been cooped up long enough, she was going to welcome the entertainment.

ABBY COULD ALMOST feel the tension in the room—it reminded her of the static electricity that filled the air before a Texas thunderstorm. The hair on her arms was literally standing on end. There was no question things would be going much differently if Carly hadn't been in the room. *Yep, ya gotta love babies.* Mentally shrugging off the heat coming her way, she decided to play offense rather than defense. She'd learned long ago when dealing with her dads and brother, proactive was a much better position than reactive.

"You all can scale back the intimidation techniques now. I'm not afraid of you, and you know as well as I do, the transponders needed to be tested. You want to know where the weaknesses are, and I did exactly what you knew I'd do... I tested it for you." She looked at Ian and caught the slight upward turn of his lips before he scuttled his expression. She zeroed in on him. "Tell me you haven't been holding back on the final patents until you knew for certain I couldn't find a way around the unit. And don't lie to me because I'll know."

This time he didn't even try to hide his grin, and he just shook his head. "Abby, you really need to rethink this path, sweetheart. I'm not denying Mitch and I knew you would test the unit because that was a given. But when you are in a hole—stop digging for heaven's sake." His words were like a pin to her balloon of self-confidence, and she suddenly felt all the starch leave her spine.

"I'm sorry. I'm just so tired of being coddled, and I miss my lab and my research and"—she took a deep breath and turned her attention from Ian to Kalen and Logan—"my new toys." She heard both men growl and saw their eyes dilate with hunger. She heard her big brother chuckle, and she wanted to kick him right in the shin. She shot him a look she hoped conveyed that message, but he didn't seem affected.

"Little sister, you can check the glare, I'm immune. As for your masterful performance, I'll let your men sort out how much of it was Oscar-worthy bullshit and how much of it was real. Right now, though, I want your happy ass in Ian's office to explain how you managed to convince my security team you were in my apartment while your car was parked in front of La Tache Couples Boutique in Alexandria."

Out of the corner of her eye, she saw both Callie's and Holly's eyes light up. *Oh brother.* It was obvious both women were delighted with the information they'd just been given. *I swear if they go without me, I'll withdraw both of their free babysitting for life passes.*

THE ONLY THING that had surprised Logan about Abby eluding their security team was it had taken so long. They'd been ready, and she'd been right about Ian stalling on the final patents. He and Kalen hadn't been too concerned because they'd asked Sergio's partner to tail her while she'd been in the city.

Abby had never met Marco Lantz, and since he was an experienced bodyguard, he'd been happy to help. Of course, the fact they didn't have to worry about Marco making a move on their woman was an added benefit as well.

Logan watched Abby stalk into Ian's office and face off with her brother. He and Kalen leaned against the wall and watched as brother and sister went toe to toe.

"It was reckless, and you know it, Abby. We're not tracking you to spy on you. Your safety and security *is* our job."

"Blow smoke up somebody else's butt, dear brother mine because it isn't working on me. I know you needed this device tested, and I did exactly that, so stop acting like I beat you at Monopoly... *again*. Geez, does Holly know you're such a big baby when you don't get your way?" Logan managed to cover his laugh with a cough, but just barely. Neither Kalen nor Gage had even tried.

"Abby, I'm warning you." Jace's threat was empty, and everybody in the room knew it. The man had a soft spot a mile wide for his little sister and always had, from what Logan had been told.

"Is that a fact? Well, big brother, bring it. Because right now, from where I stand, it seems as if I own Park Place, and it's got a couple of nice hotels on it, and you just landed there. So, it might be in your best interest to play nice with me…" Logan saw the mischief he'd always loved so much flash in her eyes just before she added, "or I'll tell mom." She stood on her tip-toes but still had to pull him down so she could kiss Jace on the cheek.

Jace groaned. "You're lucky I love you so much because you really are a pain in my ass." Then Jace focused his attention over Abby's shoulder to where he and Kalen stood. "I hope you two know what you're getting in to."

Ian straightened from where he'd been leaning against his desk. "Well, if you two are finished with your little tiff, I'd like to hear just exactly how Wonder Woman here managed to elude my security team in order to go to a kink store."

IAN HAD CALLED Mitch to sit in via video conference, and by the time Abby finished explaining how she'd managed to disrupt the tracking signal using common household items, she had wondered if the man known as an unflappable businessman wasn't going to blow a gasket. She'd gotten so caught up in the excitement of her "discovery," she'd forgotten she was explaining to one of the richest men in the free world how she'd proven his latest invention to be defective. *Oh yeah, Abby… how to make friends and influence people. Dale Carnegie would be so proud… not.*

She just sat quietly and waited while Mitch and Ian seemed to process the information she'd given them. Ian paced, and Mitch drummed his pencil so fast, it sounded like a woodpecker on speed. When Ian finally stopped and spun to face her, Abby went on full alert.

"I don't know whether I should persuade your Masters to paddle your ass or hire you. Damn." His soft laughter let her know he wasn't really angry with her, and she really was grateful for that because she liked both Ian and Mitch.

Mitch started laughing out loud, "Abby, don't let Ian fool you. He's thrilled you have pointed out a flaw in the tracker that would have caused us untold embarrassment if we'd sent it out like this. You managed to uncover a glitch our entire R & D team missed despite several months of rigorous testing. Personally, I think hiring you is a damned good idea. I've got your back on this one, sweetness. And let me add, I'm impressed as hell."

Suddenly, Abby felt like the whole room was studying her, and she didn't know why. Sure, she'd been lost in thought for several seconds, but she was considering a fix for the tracker, and she thought she had it too. But when she'd started to speak, she realized she'd become the bug under the microscope. She looked curiously around the room and then asked "What?" to no one in particular.

"Un-fucking-believable. She just solved it in under a minute. Give the girl a gold star, and I swear if you guys lay a hand on her for this, I'll put Rissa on the next plane east and leave her there for a week." Mitch's teasing tone was in direct contrast to his words and Abby relaxed.

"I'm going to see you soon, Mitch, and I'll be happy to help more with the tracker when I'm there if you have time to brainstorm with me. Please tell Rissa and Kat I am looking forward to a little girl time in the gardens. I'll let Alex and Zach know my flight information and arrival time in a couple of days." Suddenly, Abby felt as if the weight of the entire world was resting on her shoulders, and it was all because she would have to leave Kalen and Logan soon. The thought of being away from them tore at her heart, but with her job and the travel it required, she knew this was going to be her new reality.

Before he disconnected the call, Mitch said, "Sweetness, don't worry forward." Even though she understood what he was saying, she wasn't convinced his advice was applicable. She simply nodded her head, so he'd know she understood what he'd been trying to convey, then he was gone. Abby found herself staring at the blank screen for several seconds as she tried to focus on what she needed to do. The danger had passed... at least for the immediate future, and it was time to get back to work.

When she turned back to the men in the room, she noticed both Logan and Kalen glaring at their phones. She set it to the back of her mind because obviously, their everyday responsibilities were back as well. She turned to Jace and stepped into his arms.

"I'm sorry, Indy." She heard him groan as he squeezed her so hard, she squeaked.

"Short Round, you know I can't stay mad at you, but I worry about you and want you safe. Your future niece or nephew is going to need you to balance out his mama's creativity. You know how much I hated science. You're gonna have to step up, little sister."

Abby laughed because it had been a running joke her brother was a major adrenaline junkie, and all things *science* bored him to distraction. During his deployments, when she'd send him updates on what she was researching, she had started including totally left-of-center comments in the middle of the information, just to see if he actually read it. And not once had he noticed until she'd resent the same e-mail with the sentence about the dancing pink elephants highlighted.

God, I'm going to miss him.

Chapter 32

L OGAN FOLLOWED ABBY through the doors of the airport and silently fumed about the fact he had done little to hide his presence, and she still hadn't noticed she was being followed. *Damn it, she needs a fucking keeper.* He and Kalen had let her think she was leaving alone, and the sadness that had surrounded her for the last thirty-six hours had almost broken him several times. But he'd agreed with Kalen that she needed to understand how deeply she was affected by the thought of being separated from them, or she wouldn't truly understand the strength of their bond with her.

Kalen was standing to the side of the gate where they were scheduled to board. Even with his mirrored sunglasses and cap, he was easy to spot, and Logan was twice as far from him as Abby was. When Abby settled into a chair and pulled out her phone, Logan saw her shoulders slump when she checked her messages. *No baby, there are no messages from your men because they are both standing in the room with you.*

Pushing off the wall, Kalen ambled over. "She still hasn't made you?"

"Nope, and there were only a few people between us going through security. Damn, she needs a full-time bodyguard."

"Yeah or a nanny." Kalen shook his head, but Logan knew neither of them was actually angry with her. They'd had a long conversation with Jace, and their future brother-in-law had reminded them people with Abby's level of intelligence are often intensely focused on their current task, and everyday things can often be totally overlooked.

Jace told them stories about Abby working on projects with such focused intensity, his parents had finally had to intervene just to get her to eat. Her dads had forbidden her from riding her horse alone after they'd searched for her until after midnight when she was twelve. The whole ranch had been in a panic, and when they found her, she was sitting along a creek frantically typing notes into a handheld computer she'd taken on the *pleasure ride*. She'd claimed immunity from punishment because her mom had forced her to go, hoping the little bookworm would get some fresh air.

Logan and Kalen had both assured Jace they understood Abby's distraction was just a part of the whole package, and they didn't want to change her, but they did plan to do everything within their power to protect her. Watching her absentmindedly fingering their collar around her neck warmed Logan's heart. She might not recognize the gesture as significant, but it was. Logan understood her need to *touch and connect* with them and was grateful to see she shared the need he felt burning so deeply inside his soul.

When their flight was called, and the first-class passengers were boarding, they followed her onto the plane and smiled as she seemed to become uncomfortable as people began crowding in her personal space. Once they were on the plane, she finally seemed to take note they might actually be a threat. When she turned and reached up to get a pillow from the open bin above her seat, he decided it was time to play with her a bit. He trapped her small hands in his much larger one and slid the palm of his free hand over the exposed flesh between her barely-there t-shirt and low-riding jeans. He felt her start to react, but she stilled when he whispered against the shell of her ear.

"Hey, baby. Need some help with that?" Before she could respond, he slid his hand past the waistband of her jeans and into her panties. "Abby? Did your Masters give you permission to wear panties today?" He heard Kalen's growl behind him and had to bite back a chuckle. Kalen had very specifically forbidden their wayward sub from wearing panties unless one of them had personally handed them to her. His friend had never cared about them with any other sub they'd shared, but with Abby, he'd become downright militant on the subject.

"No."

Logan pulled the lobe of her ear between his teeth and applied just enough pressure to get her attention.

"Want to try that answer again, baby? Or shall I just paddle your bare little ass right here before we take off?" He felt her entire body shudder, and her pussy was instantly slick with her cream.

"No, Sir. They did not give me permission to wear them. You aren't going to tell either of them, are you? I might be willing to trade services for your silence."

Logan was glad she couldn't see the smile he hadn't been able to hold back. *Damn, I love everything about her. Her willingness to play along is going to be fun, and God knows, it is going to take both of us to keep up with her.*

"But be forewarned, my Masters are a couple of kick-ass warriors who don't share well."

Another growl from behind him from Kalen let him

know he and Abby were testing his friend's patience. Logan began circling her rapidly swelling clit and savored how responsive she was to his touch. Her panties were drenched—*serves the little wench right for wearing them*—and her breathing was rapid and shallow. With his cheek pressed against her pulse point, he could feel it pounding faster and faster.

In the back of Logan's mind, he registered Kalen was assuring the flight attendant there wasn't a problem, his brother had surprised his fiancé on the flight and was now teasing her about not noticing him on the concourse. Logan began fucking her with his fingers and barely recognized his own voice when he finally found his voice.

"Look at me, Abby." When she turned her head to look into his eyes, his breath caught at the dueling looks of relief and lust shining there. "Did you really think we were going to let you just walk away from us? That we would be willing to stay in D.C. while you traveled alone?" When the first tear breached her lower lid and rolled down her cheek, he felt the emotion pouring from her. Her heart had broken when they'd let her walk away, and now he understood why she'd seemed so distant the past few days.

He knew time was running out, and he wanted her sated and pliant in his arms, so he began applying direct pressure to her clit. "Kiss me, baby, then I want you to come for me. I want to feel your pussy squeeze my fingers as your honey runs between them." He sealed his lips over hers and pinched her clit firmly before plunging his fingers deep and curving them to press against her g-spot. Her entire body shook, and even though he'd caught her scream in their kiss, he was sure anyone near would know exactly what had just happened.

When he felt her relax in his arms, he pulled his fingers

from her and shamelessly sucked them into his mouth and licked them clean. He released her wrists and massaged her cold fingers as he turned her fully into the circle of his arms and hugged her tight.

When they were told to take their seats, he turned her to Kalen before settling her between them. Watching Kalen fasten her lap belt and kiss away the tear tracks on her cheeks as he spoke to her in soothing tones, Logan suddenly realized for the first time since the first time he'd seen a teammate die on a mission, he felt *whole* again.

His last mission as a SEAL had left him in a very dark place. He would always credit Callie McGregor with setting his healing in motion. There was a pure sense of goodness in her that had reached into the darkness and started coaxing him back into the light. But Abby was the reason he willingly stepped back into the open meadow of life. Having her between him and Kalen made everything *right*.

Chapter 33

Two weeks later

L AYING BACK IN the lounge chair, listening to the surf gently lapping at the shore, Abby thought back on the past couple of months and marveled at how much her life had changed. From the moment she and her team realized the global significance of her research results, her entire world had seemed to start spinning faster and faster out of control.

The out-of-control feeling of being caught in a snow-ball someone had pushed down a mountain hadn't stopped until she'd leaped into Kalen's arms from her cold and dark hiding place on a frigid mountainside in western Virginia. The moment his arms wrapped around her and Logan stepped up alongside her, the two men had stilled the chaos that always seemed to play inside her head.

When she'd been about ten, one of her gifted teachers had asked her what it was like inside her head. Abby had spent several minutes gathering laptops, televisions, and radios. Once she'd placed all the devices around the room, she made certain none were tuned to the same station or playing the same video. As the teacher stood in the middle with her hands over her ears, Abby had stepped up and started talking to the woman as if nothing was wrong.

The young woman's shoulders had finally sagged in defeat, and Abby had turned everything off and explained *that* was exactly what it was like in her head, except each of those broadcasts was a line of thought Abby was creating and following herself.

Not surprisingly, the woman had tendered her resignation as Abby's teacher and tutor the next day. Miss Jewel had told her parents they needed to stop fooling themselves she could continue in a mainstream classroom. She remembered her fathers had called her into their office at home and patiently explained that perhaps she should stick with verbal descriptions in the future.

Kalen's inner sense of peace always seemed to wrap itself around her psyche and pull her into a more settled place. The only way she could describe it was he took all the electrical energy bouncing around inside her and acted as a ground. He funneled it into an organized flow that made sense and was more purposeful. He balanced her.

Logan was her wild heart's other half. He made it okay to be silly, and he helped her not take herself so seriously. Logan was the gas to her fire. With him, she could be silly and flirty. He seemed to understand women in a way only a man with three older sisters would. His easy acceptance of all things "girly" made him fun and easy to be around.

The day they'd flown to Colorado, they'd had two layovers and hadn't arrived at the Lamonts' and Matthews' ShadowDance Mountain home until early evening. Abby had been shocked to see her family and friends spilling out the front door. Hearing they'd all gathered there to quickly pull together a spectacular wedding and commitment ceremony had brought her to tears more than once.

Meeting Kalen's and Jace's families had been a study in contrasts. She'd never known them to talk much about their families, so she'd been surprised to find out that both came from wealthy backgrounds and what her parents had always referred to as "old money." But she'd quickly discovered even though they were polar opposites in some ways, they were all outgoing and accepting of the unconventional lifestyle their respective sons had chosen.

The dress Callie and Holly picked out for her had literally taken her breath away. The elegance and classic lines were perfect, and its faceted embellishments reflected the fairy lights in the garden, so it sparkled as if it was electrified. The Lamonts' toddler daughter, Mary Catherine had called her a *Tinkerella*. Kat had explained that Mary Kate, as the family called her, was well known for meshing the characters from her storybooks together. Abby was sure the child was smart as a whip and likely going to give her fathers a real run for their money. Abby had thanked the little doll and assured her she did indeed feel just like a fairy princess.

Abby was startled from her thoughts by the feel of Kalen's fingers blazing a trail of fire along her exposed abdomen just above her bikini bottom. She was always amazed by the ease with which they commanded her body.

"What has that lovely smile gracing your lips, my love?" When she cautiously opened her eyes, expecting to be blinded by the sun, she was surprised to find Logan standing at her other side, so her face was shaded.

"I was thinking about how incredibly lucky I am. So many wonderful things have happened to me in the past few months, and I think it's important to recognize and appreciate the blessings we're given." She grinned at them both before adding, "And I think Mary Kate said it best because I really do feel like *Tinkerella*."

Books by Avery Gale

The ShadowDance Club
Katarina's Return – Book One
Jenna's Submission – Book Two
Rissa's Recovery – Book Three
Trace & Tori – Book Four
Reborn as Bree – Book Five
Red Clouds Dancing – Book Six
Perfect Picture – Book Seven

Club Isola
Capturing Callie – Book One
Healing Holly – Book Two
Claiming Abby – Book Three

Masters of the Prairie Winds Club
Out of the Storm
Saving Grace
Jen's Journey
Bound Treasure
Punishing for Pleasure
Accidental Trifecta
Missionary Position
Another Second Chance
Star-Crossed Miracles
Dusted Star
Lilly's Choice

The Wolf Pack Series
Mated – Book One
Fated Magic – Book Two
Tempted by Darkness – Book Three

The Knights of the Boardroom
Book One
Book Two
Book Three

The Morgan Brothers of Montana
Coral Hearts – Book One
Dancing with Deception – Book Two
Caged Songbird – Book Three
Game On – Book Four
Well Bred – Book Five

Mountain Mastery
Well Written
Savannah's Sentinel
Sheltering Reagan

Enchanted Holidays
The Christmas Painting

I would love to hear from you!

Website:
www.averygale.com

Facebook:
facebook.com/avery.gale.3

Twitter:
@avery_gale

www.ingramcontent.com/pod-product-compliance
Lightning Source LLC
Chambersburg PA
CBHW060914180626
46817CB00004B/1249